The Demon Sword Master of Excalibur Academy

[6]

Yu Shimizu

ILLUSTRATION
Asagi Tosaka

NEW YORK

Yu Shimizu

Translation by Roman Lempert
Cover art by Asagi Tosaka

This book is a work of fiction. Names, characters, places, and incidents are the product of the author's imagination or are used fictitiously. Any resemblance to actual events, locales, or persons, living or dead, is coincidental.

SEIKEN GAKUIN NO MAKEN TSUKAI Volume 6
©Yu Shimizu 2021
First published in Japan in 2021 by KADOKAWA CORPORATION, Tokyo.
English translation rights arranged with KADOKAWA CORPORATION, Tokyo, through TUTTLE-MORI AGENCY, INC., Tokyo.

English translation © 2022 by Yen Press, LLC

Yen Press, LLC supports the right to free expression and the value of copyright. The purpose of copyright is to encourage writers and artists to produce the creative works that enrich our culture.

The scanning, uploading, and distribution of this book without permission is a theft of the author's intellectual property. If you would like permission to use material from the book (other than for review purposes), please contact the publisher. Thank you for your support of the author's rights.

Yen On
150 West 30th Street, 19th Floor
New York, NY 10001

Visit us at yenpress.com
facebook.com/yenpress ★ twitter.com/yenpress
yenpress.tumblr.com ★ instagram.com/yenpress

First Yen On Edition: June 2022
Edited by Yen On Editorial: Jordan Blanco
Designed by Yen Press Design: Liz Parlett

Yen On is an imprint of Yen Press, LLC.
The Yen On name and logo are trademarks of Yen Press, LLC.

The publisher is not responsible for websites (or their content) that are not owned by the publisher.

Library of Congress Cataloging-in-Publication Data
Names: Shimizu, Yu, author. | Tosaka, Asagi, illustrator. | Lempert, Roman, translator.
Title: The demon sword master of Excalibur Academy / Yu Shimizu ; illustration by Asagi Tosaka ; translation by Roman Lempert.
Other titles: Seiken gakuin no maken tsukai. English
Description: First Yen On edition. | New York : Yen On, 2020.
Identifiers: LCCN 2020017005 | ISBN 9781975308667 (v. 1 ; trade paperback) | ISBN 9781975319151 (v. 2 ; trade paperback) | ISBN 9781975320706 (v. 3 ; trade paperback) | ISBN 9781975320720 (v. 4 ; trade paperback) | ISBN 9781975335427 (v. 5 ; trade paperback) | ISBN 9781975343460 (v. 6 ; trade paperback)
Subjects: CYAC: Fantasy. | Demonology—Fiction. | Reincarnation—Fiction
Classification: LCC PZ7.1.S5174 De 2020 | DDC [Fic]—dc23
LC record available at https://lccn.loc.gov/2020017005

ISBNs: 978-1-9753-4346-0 (paperback)
978-1-9753-4347-7 (ebook)

1 3 5 7 9 10 8 6 4 2

LSC-C

Printed in the United States of America

Contents

The Demon Sword Master of Excalibur Academy

Prologue		p001
Chapter 1	The Dark Lord Zol Vadis	p005
Chapter 2	The Kenki Gathering	p027
Chapter 3	Tessera's Birthday Party	p047
Chapter 4	Intruder in the Dark Lord's Castle	p069
Chapter 5	The Dark Lord Explores the Sakura Orchid	p085
Chapter 6	The Twin Gods	p099
Chapter 7	The Enshrinement Ritual	p115
Chapter 8	Setsura	p139
Chapter 9	The Mightiest Swordmaster	p159
Chapter 10	Holy Sword Awakening	p175
Epilogue		p195

PROLOGUE

One thousand years ago...

In Las Olzande, a corrupt land on the frontier of the Kingdom of Rognas, there stood two figures, each of them emanating an unusual presence.

"Please step back, Sir Gisark. I will handle this," one of them said quietly.

He was a great man, boasting an impressive, toned physique. His shining, golden hair extended down to his waist, and his eyes were as black as unfathomable darkness. He wore a pure white overcoat and clutched a broadsword as tall as he was.

He was Shardark Shin Ignis. A ray of hope for humanity, chosen by the Luminous Powers themselves. The Six Heroes' strongest Swordmaster.

"He was your disciple. Can you truly cut him down?" questioned the other figure, a warrior with the head of a dragon.

Armor seemingly crafted of scales protected him, and he carried a pair of single-edged blades. This was the Divine Dragon of the Six Heroes, Gisark Saint Dragon.

"Of course. That disciple of mine has fallen to darkness, and I will personally deliver him from this mortal realm."

With his sword in hand, Shardark gazed at the army of undead along the horizon. Not a single living creature stood among the ranks. There were only the unliving remains of tens of thousands of Rognas soldiers, all of them animated and controlled by vast amounts of mana.

And the one leading that legion of the dead on the back of a massive black wolf was none other than the Undead King—Leonis Death Magnus. Soaring above it all was an army of wyrms commanded by a gigantic red dragon.

"Sir Gisark, you handle that one—"

"Veira, the Dragon Lord, eh? That one's obsessed with killing me." Gisark had slain the dragons roosting on the Demon Dragon's Mountain Range, devouring them all. "Very well. It's about time I consumed that girl, too."

Gisark transformed into a great silvery wyrm and soared up into the clouds. After watching his companion take flight, Shardark leaped into the air.

"My most unworthy disciple, who succumbed to the Goddess of Rebellion's cajolery... This is where I put an end to you!"

Whooooooosh!

Shardark's greatsword gouged into the earth, loosing a luminous shockwave that swept away the armies of the dead. Yet the Undead King was unperturbed, merely sneering.

"I am afraid that is impossible, my master. I have long since surpassed you."

The Undead King hurled a wave of dark mana. Its thick miasma swallowed and rotted the land as it raced forward, washing over the hero.

"—You would do well not to underestimate the Swordmaster!"

Fighting spirit surged from Shardark's body like a torrent of light, extinguishing his opponent's attack.

"Dark Lord Leonis! You have fallen from the just path, and for that, I shall destroy you!"

In Shardark's hands was one of the Arc Seven, Oborozuki. The great weapon's blade shone with the power to crush all evil.

"Prepare to join the ranks of my undead army, ye champion of mankind!" the Undead King declared.

A storm of destruction raged across the lifeless scenery.

CHAPTER 1

 THE DARK LORD ZOL VADIS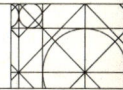

"Leo... Just *who are you?*"

Riselia's blue eyes, as clear as a lake's surface, gazed at Leonis. It was nine in the evening when, just as Leonis was speaking with Blackas, Riselia had come to see him. In her hands was a scrap of paper, a copy of an epitaph found on a statue in Necrozoa. Riselia had decoded the writing and discovered that someone named Leonis Death Magnus had been the ruler of that long-forgotten dark region.

"E-erm..." Leonis clearly averted his gaze and swallowed nervously.

How did she manage to read an ancient, mystic text?!

The Dark Lord in the body of a ten-year-old gritted his teeth, annoyed by his own carelessness. He ought to have destroyed that inscription discreetly. Leonis knew of Riselia's fervent interest when it came to researching ancient ruins, after all. But he never imagined she would successfully decode the language.

Wasn't the ancient script wiped from the history books?!

Apparently, Riselia had translated Leonis's name using a book she'd found in her father's study. Duke Crystalia had been a scholar of age-old relics, as well. Still, to think his daughter would decipher the writing so quickly…

Some part of Leonis wanted to praise this minion of his for her resourcefulness, but now certainly wasn't the time.

Until now, Leonis maintained the lie that he was an ancient mage who had awoken in this age. And if this honest girl, with her stern sense of justice, were to learn that Leonis was actually a Dark Lord, there was no telling how she might react.

Will she respond as the humans did back then…? No, she's…

Leonis bit his lips for a moment, and then…

"It appears you've found me out. Very well, then," he whispered with self-derision.

"Leo…?" Riselia's blue eyes wavered anxiously.

Forgive me, but I must wipe your memories of this.

Fortunately, manipulating this one simple recollection wouldn't have any effect on her personality. Leonis reached out his hands to touch Riselia's temple.

"Leo—"

Before the Dark Lord could do any more, his minion abruptly wrapped her arms around him.

"Miss…Selia?"

"I'm your guardian, Leo, so I want to know everything about you. But if there's something you don't want to share, I won't force you. I can be okay with that, even if you're not who I think you are, so…!"

Riselia's argent locks brushed against Leonis's cheek. Feeling her hold him tight, Leonis let his arms drop, putting them around her instead.

I shouldn't be altering my minion's memory.

For some reason, a part of him knew that it would irrevocably alter their relationship forever if he were to try it.

"It's true. I once ruled that ruined city, back when it was still Necrozoa," Leonis admitted, sitting on the bed beside Riselia.

He'd elected to tell the truth and revealed that he was once master of a kingdom of countless skeletons and demons.

"...So you really were a king."

"Yes, well..." Leonis nodded sheepishly, scratching his cheek. "That land eventually met its demise."

"...How?"

"There were many reasons, but, well..." Leonis's shoulders slumped. "Simply put, I suppose my reign left something to be desired. That's probably why..."

"So you're trying to rebuild that kingdom?"

"...No. It's already been destroyed."

This wasn't to say he didn't feel any nostalgia for Necrozoa, but that place had only ever been a military base for the Dark Lords' Armies. Leonis's home was wherever the goddess Roselia was.

Besides, I already have a new headquarters...

"What matters most now is finding someone very important to me," Leonis said.

"You mean the lady you talked about once?"

"Yes. Roselia Ishtaris. Locating her is my—"

"Roselia... Isn't that...?" Riselia interjected. "I saw that name on the epitaph."

"You decoded her name, too?!" Leonis exclaimed, shocked.

"Y-yes..."

"I—I see...," Leonis whispered, almost impressed.

Evidently, he still underestimated Riselia's passion for historical research.

"Is that lady a mage like you, Leo?"

"No, she's..." Leonis paused to consider. "In the present era, she's likely an ordinary girl."

◆

After Riselia had left the room, Leonis sat alone for a moment—but then his shadow began stirring and wavering.

"That was quite dangerous, Lord Magnus."

A massive, pitch-black wolf rose from his shadow. It was Blackas.

The dignified beast climbed onto Leonis's bed and snorted slightly. "Why didn't you wipe that girl's memory?"

"It was unnecessary. Altering her mind every time she began to suspect something would have grown tiresome."

"Hmm." Blackas appeared unconvinced.

Leonis sighed and shrugged. "Rewriting the memories of my minions shames my honor as a Dark Lord."

"Your dignity, you say. It's not my place to comment on it, then."

In the end, Leonis didn't tell Riselia he was a Dark Lord. He couldn't share the truth with her yet.

But someday, I'll reveal everything to her.

Now wasn't that time, though. When he brought Roselia's reincarnation under his protection and reformed the Dark Lords' Armies, he would tell her.

Straightening up, Leonis cleared his throat. "More importantly, there is something I'm curious about."

"What is it?" the black wolf asked.

"Riselia discovered some writing in her father's study that aided her in translating writing in Necrozoa. But how would Duke Crystalia, a man from this age, know of the ancient text?"

The epitaph on the statue hadn't been described in just any dead language. It had been written in the advanced holy text, a script employed exclusively by the wisest, most esteemed priests.

"Duke Crystalia studied ancient history, but that he was aware of legends surrounding the Dark Lords still feels very curious. It's a shame he's already dead...," muttered Leonis.

The Holy Woman, Tearis Resurrectia, had been revived in the ruins of the Third Assault Garden as a Void Lord, turning the souls of the dead knights into wandering spirits. However, Leonis hadn't located Duke Crystalia's soul when he'd been there.

The Undead King put a hand to his chin as he mused ominously, "If I could at least find the body, I could use necromancy to resurrect him as a ghoul..."

An Excalibur Academy unit was investigating the half-destroyed ruins of the Third Assault Garden, but it wasn't likely that any corpses would turn up.

"Setting that aside...," Leonis said. Another matter weighed on his mind. Namely, what was Zemein, a staff officer of the Dark Lords' Armies, doing in Necrozoa? "Zemein and Nefakess Reizaad. Members of the old Dark Lords' Armies seem to be scheming in the shadows."

When Leonis fought Zemein in Necrozoa's Goddess Temple, he had spoken of a prophecy.

A presage, eh...?

Leonis knew of one the goddess Roselia had made, stating she would be reborn in this era. Was there yet another prophecy, then?

"I found Zemein in Necrozoa, trying to resurrect me—the Undead King. He was likely hoping to taint me with the power of nothingness and turn me into a Void Lord, just like they did with Veira and the Six Heroes." Had Riselia not accidentally undone the seal on him, that plan could very well have come to fruition.

"They're trying to use the Six Heroes and the Dark Lords to suit their ends."

Who was masterminding these acts? Leonis suspected the Devil of the Underworld, Azra-Ael, might be the one pulling the strings, but Zemein had denied that. There was nothing that kept him from lying, however.

"Zemein dying was an unfortunate loss, though," Leonis admitted.

While Leonis had been questioning Zemein, a masked girl had appeared and destroyed the old man. Even Leonis, with his mastery over death magic, couldn't call back a soul that had been completely eradicated. At best, he could manipulate Zemein's corpse like one might a puppet, but it would provide no information.

I can't help but feel like that woman reminded me of someone...

"My lord..."

The shadow at Leonis's feet began to undulate again, and a girl in a maid's dress rose from it. It was Shary, the assassin maid.

"Yes, Shary, what is it?"

"I come bearing an urgent report, my lord," Shary stated, pinching up her skirt in a dignified curtsy.

"Oh? What is it?"

"Your Demon Wolf Pack minions have begun acting on their own again."

"Again...?" Leonis sighed and massaged his temples wearily.

The Demon Wolf Pack was a group composed of remnants of the Sovereign Wolves, a terrorist organization that had hijacked the royal family's private craft, the *Hyperion*. They were the first subordinates Leonis had gathered since awakening from stasis, excluding Riselia, his personal servant.

Many of the beastmen in the group were quite bloodthirsty and impulsive, and just the other day, they had attacked a research facility in the Sixth Assault Garden, which got them caught up in Veira's rampage.

Their loyalty to their new Dark Lord master was high, but they were a constant source of vexation for Leonis.

"What did they do this time?"

"They infiltrated a naval pier and are planning to steal weapons."

"..."

Needless to say, Leonis had not ordered them to do that.

"...My word, handling them is nothing like commanding the undead." Leonis sighed again.

"What shall we do, my lord?" Shary asked.

"I'll go stop them." Leonis got to his feet, produced a skull mask from thin air, and put it on.

Shadows enveloped his whole body, disguising Leonis as a tall demon clad in a long overcoat. He took this form, that of the Dark Lord Zol Vadis, when meeting with the Demon Wolf Pack.

The ten-year-old boy attending Excalibur Academy was merely Leonis's public front. This masked persona was the dark master controlling the Seventh Assault Garden from behind the scenes.

◆

"The boat just docked in the port. How are things on your end?"

"All green. I silenced the soldiers standing guard."

"Roger. We'll get into the warehouse, then."

The dark elf girl Lena silenced her communication device. She and the others were in the Seventh Assault Garden's military pier area on Port 04. This massive armory housed a large amount of anti-Void weapons and ammunition.

The sky was quite cloudy, blotting out the moon. However, the low-hanging clouds reflected the illumination from the numerous searchlights, revealing things.

Several shadows clinging to the rooftops silently descended to the ground. They wore hoods that hung over their eyes and masks that covered their faces as they sprinted under the veil of darkness.

They were the remnants of the Sovereign Wolves, a group of anti-imperial terrorists made up mostly of beastmen. Currently, they functioned as the operative unit of the Demon Wolf Pack, an organization working under Zol Vadis.

Having caught wind of information that a ship loaded with military equipment was about to dock, they plotted to loot the warehouse in an attempt to acquire weapons and ammo.

Ugh. I'm a hero, for heaven's sake! Why am I skulking about like some kind of sneak thief?

Squatting next to Lena, one girl with verdant hair puffed out her cheeks with displeasure. She was a beautiful young lady, her eyes a mystical shade of blue. Although she appeared no older than thirteen or fourteen, the air about her gave the impression of a keen, honed blade.

Arle Kirlesio was an elven hero dispatched by the Elder Tree. Her goal was to fell the Goddess of Rebellion, who would supposedly make a return in this era, as well as the Dark Lords serving her.

Yet during a scuffle when Arle had been pursued by the local guards, she'd been picked up by these terrorists. And as she remained with them, she came to learn that their leader called himself a Dark Lord.

Zol Vadis.

That was the name of a Dark Lord who'd governed nearly the entire world before the advent of the Goddess of Rebellion. After which Zol Vadis was slain by the hero Leonis Shealto. Arle decided to remain with the Demon Wolf Pack to discover their master's true identity, but unfortunately, she hadn't yet risen to a rank where she was permitted to meet him.

Thus, to that end, she had to prove her strength and gain admittance into the organization's inner circle.

"This plan was your idea, wasn't it?" she asked Lena. "The Dark Lord—I mean, His Greatness—didn't order you to do this, right?"

"Yes, that's right." Lena nodded boastfully for some reason. "His Greatness said, 'I expect loyalty from my subordinates, but not the kind of blind adherence skeletons or zombies have.' In other words, His Greatness expects us to think and act on our own."

Lena explained this proudly, holding up an index finger.

"That's why we're doing this, elf girl," one of the beastmen added.

It seemed the Demon Wolf Pack's members were all genuinely loyal to this Dark Lord.

Arle hung her head and silently muttered an incantation for a night vision spell. She could see vehicles ferrying large container boxes into the warehouse.

Boom, boom, booooooooooom!

Suddenly, a series of rumbling explosions shook the air. It was a distraction caused by another detachment of the Demon Wolf Pack.

"Let's go, Arle!" Lena said enthusiastically.

"...Yes, fine," Arle replied lackadaisically, placing her hand on the Arc Seven sword she carried.

Five shadows hopped from one roof to the next under cover of night.

The beastmen's stamina is impressive.

A thousand years ago, the majority of the beastmen were united under one of the Dark Lords, Gazoth Grand Beast. The beastmen of that age fought with mighty physiques and sharp claws, striking fear into the kingdom's allies. And it seemed their overwhelming physical abilities had survived to the present era.

Arle kicked off and jumped ahead of the beastmen.

"Stand back. I'll handle the guards."

"Huh?! Hey, newbie, are you trying to hog all the glory?!" one hulking lion-headed beastman snarled at her.

"That wasn't my intent."

"Stop, let her go," Lena said calmly, diffusing the beastman's anger. "It's a good chance to see what she's capable of."

"...If you say so," the lion-headed beastman said.

"That's enough chatter, then. Arle, show us what an elven swordfighter can do."

"All right," Arle replied, drawing her sword and dropping from the warehouse's roof.

One guard wearing night vision goggles turned around to face her, pointing his anti-Void rifle at her.

"Wh-what?! Who are you?!"

Arle had already finished chanting her spell, however. "Spirits of slumber, whisper your lullabies—Sleep!"

Mana vapor covered the area, knocking out all the guards in front of her.

"Intruder...call for rein—"

A few of those on patrol resisted the sleep spell and tried calling for help, but Arle's blade flashed before they could. The sword streaked through the air swifter than the guards' voices, cutting them down one by one. Naturally, she used the blunt side of her weapon. She landed dry blows that knocked them unconscious.

Arle had cast a blade-dulling spell on her Arc Seven, ensuring that she could end this without needless bloodshed.

Still, this isn't something a hero should do, she thought, heart full of guilt and self-loathing.

What would the Elder Tree in her homeland think if it knew of this? And more importantly, what would her teacher, the Swordmaster of the Six Heroes, think?

"Color me surprised." Lena landed behind her and whistled as if impressed. "You really took them out all on your own."

"Will I be admitted as a close associate of His Greatness now?"

Lena shook her head. "Not quite yet."

Arle shrugged.

"None of these guards seems to be wielding Holy Swords."

"They wouldn't have anti-Void combat elites guard a warehouse," Lena replied.

Arle stood in front of the large warehouse's special alloy bulkhead.

"Opening this is my part." Lena stepped forward and took out a hacking terminal. "I'll unlock the door."

"That's unnecessary," Arle stated.

"Huh?"

A flash of her sword, and the sturdy bulkhead split in two and fell away.

"...What?!" Lena cried in disbelief. The others were similarly shocked. "Impossible. This is a military-grade, special mithril steel door! It's built to withstand a Void attack!"

"This sword can cut through Orichalcum with ease," Arle whispered curtly. Then she stepped into the warehouse. "Let's go."

Countless freight containers formed tall rows inside. It was pitch black, but the beastmen's night vision would likely make the loading work go smoothly.

"Which boxes have the weapons?" Arle questioned. "We can't take all of them."

"We don't know. For now, we'll have to open them and search," Lena replied.

Arle gave an exasperated look.

"Raaaaah!" One burly werebear swung his claws, tearing a container's flank open.

"Heh-heh-heh, now let's see what treasure we have in this chest...," said the werebear, smacking his lips as he tore the container's walls open. "Huh? Wait... What's this?"

"What's wrong, Bertuma?" Lena asked as she approached.

"...Wait!" Arle called out. Struck by an ominous feeling, she grabbed Lena by the shoulder and pulled her back. No sooner had she done so than a squelching sound, like a fruit being crushed, filled the warehouse.

"...?!"

The young werebear's head vanished. His limbs dangled limply as his lifeless frame was cast high into the air.

"Wha... Bertuma...!"

R-riiiiiiiiiiiip!

The container walls were torn from the inside, and the awful sound reverberated. The *thing* that emerged from within was a humanoid. Its black silhouette possessed elongated limbs.

Wh-what is this...?!

By Arle's reckoning, it resembled a knight in full armor. Red eyes glinted from within its helmet, and an inky miasma blew out from the seams in its armor.

"Isn't that one of the anti-Void combat protection suits they use in the polar regions?" Lena remarked as she assumed a combat stance.

"Boss lady, is that one of the weapons we're supposed to steal?" a beastman asked as he, too, adopted a fighting pose.

"So there's someone inside that thing?" another beastman inquired.

"That doesn't matter anymore, not after it killed Bertuma," declared the lion-headed beastman, swinging his claws up. "Waste it!"

"Shaz, stop!" Lena insisted, but he had already pounced on the armored foe.

Vaaaaaaaaaaaah...!

The armor burst from the inside, and a terrifying amount of oily vapor spewed from within it. Something appeared in the darkness, and after glimpsing its form—

"Wh-what...?!"

"H-hey, isn't that...?!"

—the beastmen's voices grew tinged with fear. A monster slithered out from within the armor. Its head was unnaturally swollen, and countless teeth protruded all over its limbs.

As it straightened up, a miasma swirled around its body.

"...A Void." Arle narrowed her eyes.

Voids were the enemies of humanity, perhaps even the entire planet. They had appeared abruptly only several decades ago, a near millennium after her native time. These were neither the monsters of the Dark Lords' Armies, nor were they demons. Voids were unknown creatures that never existed in the old world.

"Hey, what the hell's going on here?! Are you telling me they smuggled Voids into this city?!"

"That can't be—"

The beastmen were confused.

An impatient weretiger fired his machine gun. "Dammit, I'll blow you away!"

Unfortunately, the Void's armor-like skin deflected the bullets effortlessly.

"No good, it's not making a dent in it!"

"Conventional weaponry doesn't work against Voids!" Lena chided him.

The Void swung down an arm, the mere shock of the blow enough to cleave the weretiger in two.

"...!"

"It's dangerous! Run!" Arle stepped forward with the Holy Sword Crozax gripped in her hands.

She'd already fought monsters like this one in the ruined city. Different specimens possessed distinct abilities, but humans and beastmen were powerless against even the smallest of them.

The Void howled and brought its arm up again.

"Ominous wind...!"

A powerful barrier of air enveloped Arle as she stepped forward, her blade glinting as it arced, cutting off the Void's arm. The dark miasma splattered into the surrounding gloom like blood.

"Arle!" Lena shouted after her fellow elf.

"I'll handle this," Arle replied as she slashed at the monster again. "You lead everyone else out of here."

"The dark elves of Darkwood never abandon a comrade!" Lena insisted.

"Forgive me for saying this, but all you'll do is hold me back. I can't fight if I have to worry about protecting you," Arle stated curtly. "But in exchange, if I get out of this, induct me into His Greatness's inner circle."

Lena bit her lip and nodded. "Tch. Fine! Just don't do anything crazy. Everyone, we fall back! Arle will hold the enemy off!"

"Y-yeah...!"

Lena made for the warehouse's exit with the beastmen in tow.

I really am too softhearted for my own good. The elven hero sighed as she slashed into the Void that was charging at her.

She had no obligation to rescue a Dark Lord's subordinates.

I am somewhat in their debt, though.

In particular, Arle felt she owed Lena. If that dark elf girl wasn't there to help her, Arle might have starved to death in some back alley. A thousand years ago, the elves and dark elves were irreconcilable enemies, so the fact a dark elf was aiding her felt unusual to the point of near impossibility.

"Come, monster," Arle taunted the enemy, holding up the Demon Smiting Sword Crozax. "You will sample the blade techniques passed down to me by the Swordmaster of the Six Heroes himself!"

With that shout, she cut the Void clean through. No sooner had she done so, however, than her long ears caught a shrill, high-frequency noise.

A War Cry.

It was a Void ability that enabled them to force the rest of their Hive to hatch. This was elementary Void knowledge, and any Excalibur Academy student would've known it, but Arle, who had only recently awakened in this era, was ignorant of the sound's meaning.

"Wh-what?"

And the next moment...

Crunch, crunch, crunch, crunch...!

The containers all ruptured at once, and more Voids appeared from within them.

"N-no...!"

Once again filled with portentous dread, Arle turned to see scores of the monsters slithering from the crates stacked up near the entrance.

There are too many of them!

Countless crimson glares shone in the night like haunted will-o'-the-wisps...and charged at her at once.

Vaaaaaaaaaaah!

"...Insolent creatures...!"

Arle swung the Demon Smiting Sword, severing the head of the first Void to reach her. The aberrant things weren't fazed in the slightest, though, and continued their advance.

"This can't be...where I...!"

Then, from somewhere unseen, a flash of lightning cut through the dark—

Huh?

—and the Voids' skulls went flying into the air. A white bolt sped across the floor, leaving the faint scent of ozone in its wake. A small figure landed on the ground with a gentle tap of their shoes. They stood clad in a beautiful white outfit, hair an electrifying shade of blue.

A slender girl wielded a katana crackling with lightning.

◆

"What's this? I thought I sensed Voids here...," the girl said, knitting her fair brows.

She's...! Arle's eyes widened in shock.

The elf recognized her savior. She was one of the Excalibur Academy students Arle had temporarily fought alongside within the ruined city. Arle had an exceptionally high opinion of this young lady, as the two had crossed blades in combat. She couldn't recall her last name, but her first name was...

Sakuya, I believe...

The young woman with the lightning sword seemed to recognize Arle as well.

"Aren't you...the elf we met in the Third Assault Garden? What are you doing here?"

"E-er..."

Arle couldn't very well tell her she was helping terrorists pillage weapons.

"L-let's defeat these monsters first!" she exclaimed, leveling her blade at the Voids surrounding them.

Sakuya shrugged. "Right," she responded, holding up her weapon and moving into Arle's flank. "Humanoid Voids are highly intelligent. Don't get careless."

"...Understood."

Arle had fought shoulder to shoulder with Sakuya only once before, but she knew the other girl was very talented and skilled. Together, they had a chance of surviving. Sakuya and Arle synced up their breathing and moved at once.

"Aaaaaaaaaah!"

"Let's go, Raikirimaru!"

As soon as Sakuya took a step forward, sparks flew. She raced ahead, charging into the heart of the Void formation. Spying this from the corner of her eye, Arle watched Sakuya with surprise.

She couldn't follow her movements. All Arle could make out were flashes of electricity crisscrossing through the dark.

Is this her true power?!

Enveloping her blade in lightning was only a by-product of Sakuya's power. Her Holy Sword's true ability was continual acceleration.

"Wind, heed my call and unleash your powers—Winde Rotso!"

Razor-sharp air cleaved through the room. This second-order fae magic spell sheared off a Void's arm.

"Hyaaaaaaaa!"

Arle then swung the Demon Smiting Sword down, charging its blade with mana. Crozax was an Arc Seven, a weapon produced by the Luminous Powers to slay Dark Lords. As such, when fighting anything else, its edge was only as keen as any other sword. This was why Arle charged it with her mana.

The Void's dying cry reverberated against the warehouses.

"I'll tear open a way out. Follow me!" Arle shouted at Sakuya.

"Oh, you just run for now. I'll stay here and exterminate the Voids."

"...?! What are you saying?! There's too many!"

"I am a swordswoman of the Sakura Orchid. I will never turn my back on Voids."

"...Huh?!"

Keen, dangerous bloodlust surged out from Sakuya's body as she slew another Void.

"You're thinking of staying?!"

"You should leave. Whenever I fight Voids, I lose sight of what's around me."

Sakuya's katana streaked like a bolt from the heavens, tearing through a metal container. As she moved, her white attire billowing, she appeared like nothing short of a maddened, demonic warrior.

Wh-what is that girl...? Some kind of berserker?!

Arle had little time to ponder the idea, however. Her sensitive ears twitched. Some kind of gigantic monster crept out of the container Sakuya had destroyed.

Vwooooooooooooooohm!

It blew off the large warehouse's roof.

"*Grrrrrrrrrrrrr...!*"

A gigantic bipedal Void stood up.

Shock was plain on Arle's face. "Voids can get that large...?!"

"That's an ogre-class." Sakuya turned to face the young elf. "If that thing were to reach the urban area, it would be catastrophic."

"And you intend to defeat this thing?"

"Fighting it off single-handedly would be difficult, I admit," Sakuya replied with an indomitable grin while holding up Raikirimaru. "I'll just have to stall for time until the academy's anti-Void unit arrives."

Arle nodded. "...I understand." As a hero, she couldn't let that thing reach civilians.

If we only have to delay it, we should be able to...

But then, something Arle didn't expect occurred.

"Who permitted you to wreak havoc in my domain? Die, lowly monster."

Vroooooooooooooooooom!

Raging fireballs rained down on the gigantic Void. Columns of crimson flame erupted so that nothing else around was visible.

"What...?!"

"...?!"

Arle and Sakuya both froze up at the sight.

"What in the world just...?!"

They both looked up, and there they saw it.

A grand demon, clad in a pitch-black overcoat, was peering down arrogantly.

◆

A red inferno lit up the night as shrill sirens blared across the pier. His fifth-order spell, Inferno Wave, was fire magic with a large area of effect, capable of reducing a troll's bones to ashes.

Why are there Voids here? Leonis cocked an eyebrow under his Dark Lord's mask.

Following Shary's report, he'd come here to stop the Demon Wolf Pack from their reckless, unauthorized operation. Yet he found Voids rampaging in their place.

For the time being, he decided to eliminate the eyesores.

But that said, those two...

Leonis detected two familiar figures among the wreckage. One of them was Arle Kirlesio, a hero of the elves. Her being here didn't come as a significant surprise. He knew that, for whatever reason, she was currently part of the Demon Wolf Pack. Her objective was likely to assassinate the Dark Lord leading them. The more curious presence was the other one.

What's Sakuya doing here?

Sakuya glared up at Leonis, Holy Sword in hand. And as he met her gaze with a confused expression shielded by his mask...

"Who are you?" Sakuya demanded with a tone that, while calm, shook the air with the sheer enmity it contained.

She didn't look like her usual self. Her eyes were full of a terrifying coldness.

Wh-what do I do now? Leonis frantically wondered as he tried to conjure up an appropriate solution. *Just calm down. They don't know who you are.*

At present, Leonis didn't look like a ten-year-old boy, but a dark being who commanded this city in secret—the Dark Lord Zol Vadis. The Mantle of Illusions he'd stolen from an ancient demon allowed him to both alter his appearance and befuddle how others perceived him. His cover wasn't easily blown.

In that case...

"I am the Dark Lord Zol Vadis," Leonis exclaimed to the two with a flourish of his mantle. "He who reigns over this city from the shadows!"

"...Wh... What?!" Arle shouted, her ears twitching in surprise. "You're...the Dark Lord...?"

"You reign over this city from the shadows?!" Sakuya repeated, her voice full of dignified anger.

"Indeed. The Seventh Assault Garden is already my domain," Leonis fibbed and brandished his arms grandly.

He didn't mind declaring that much. Stating a Dark Lord's name didn't strike him as a bad idea.

"...So it was you? You were the one who smuggled these Voids into the city?"

"What?" Leonis scowled.

Smuggled was an interesting way of phrasing it. Leonis had thought Voids emerged from cracks in space.

"Are you implying I called these Voids to wipe them out myself?" Leonis questioned.

Sakuya faltered slightly. "Uh, well..."

"These despicable creatures are naught but enemies of mine," Leonis explained, lording over the two girls from above. "The Seventh Assault Garden belongs to me and my forces. I won't let these hollow monstrosities do as they wish in my domain."

Arle reached for the Demon Smiting Sword but stopped herself. She realized that challenging the Dark Lord here would mean one-sided defeat. Sakuya, meanwhile, kept her narrowed eyes trained on Leonis with Raikirimaru at the ready.

Fortunately, the thrum of approaching footsteps broke the stalemate.

"It seems Excalibur Academy's forces are approaching..."

Sakuya turned to look.

"I bid you adieu for tonight," Leonis said. "I have pressing matters I must attend to."

With a wave of his mantle, Leonis made to leave. He had homework due tomorrow, after all.

"W-wait...!" Sakuya's voice echoed through the night. But the Dark Lord Zol Vadis was already gone.

CHAPTER 2

THE KENKI GATHERING

A battle was underway in one of Excalibur Academy's training areas.

"Lightning, gouge my foes—Vil Valut!"

Magical electricity wreathed the tip of Riselia's crimson, shining blade. Riselia, wearing her training wear, swung the Bloody Sword, searing the air.

"Hm, so the Holy Sword, this supernatural power of yours, can also conduct spells. Interesting," the skeletal mage instructing her remarked quietly as he thrust out the staff gripped in his bony hands.

The end of the staff shone and dispelled the lightning around the blade. The skeleton was Nefisgal, the Underworld's Archmage, one of the Three Champions of Rognas, and a servant of Leonis.

"Well, it may help you blind an enemy, should the need arise," Nefisgal commented.

"I-I'm not done yet!" Riselia called out.

She dashed forward, closing the distance between her and the skeleton. As she ran, the young woman intoned another spell.

"Sweep over all, raging blade of gales—Jiura Kires!"

Riselia's swipe loosed an invisible blade of compressed air.

"The Vampire Queen's power is indeed impressive," Nefisgal praised as he batted Riselia's attack away. "You already possess vast reserves of mana."

The statement wasn't an empty compliment for his liege's minion. As the highest rank of undead, Riselia's latent mana potential exceeded even that of an elder lich like Nefisgal.

"However..." The skeleton wagged a bony finger. "The composition of your spells is still lacking, leaving your abundance of mana as an untapped treasure. Of course, being able to learn first-order spells after just a few days of training is impressive enough."

Nefisgal raised his staff again, and the space around Riselia twisted in response. This was a second-order gravity spell, the Gravity Distortion Field, Divan Zo.

"Aaah...!" Riselia cried as she lost her balance and was slammed hard against the training facility's floor. "Khhk...!"

"N-Nefisgal, try to be gentler with her...!" Leonis, who'd been leaning against the wall and watching over the session, protested in concern.

"I-I'm fine... Leo..." Riselia rose to her feet with some effort, holding up the Bloody Sword. "Please, give me more!"

"You heard her, my lord. Shall I continue?" Nefisgal turned to Leonis, who cracked a forced smile and shrugged.

Perhaps I really am being overly protective of her.

Riselia was the one who'd requested that they teach her sorcery. Indeed, vampires mostly fought by weaving spells with their vast mana reserves. And under the tutelage of Leonis and Nefisgal, two accomplished sorcerers, Riselia matured at a fast pace.

She has genuine promise. One day I shall have her lead my followers as my right hand. And speaking of minions...

Leonis thought back to the night prior. Based on the report

Shary had given him earlier that day, the Demon Wolf Pack had plotted to steal weapons from the pier. But instead of arms and equipment, the containers were loaded with Voids.

But why? Leonis pondered. *Why would Voids, enemies of humanity, be in a military harbor?*

He'd never believed keeping Voids in captivity was possible. During the fight in the Third Assault Garden, Leonis had trapped a few in the Realm of Shadows, but they all dissipated like fog before long.

And then there's the matter of Sakuya.

Why had she been there?

My word. It's one answerless question after another.

Things had undoubtedly grown more complicated in the past one thousand years. Back then, might had been everything.

◆

For the hour that followed, training continued until Riselia couldn't keep going anymore.

"Truly, she is my lord's minion. Her talent is as rare as it is astounding," Nefisgal said.

"She is indeed remarkable," Leonis agreed, nodding at the skeletal archmage's words.

"However, her control over her mana still requires improvement," Nefisgal continued.

"Well, I wouldn't fault her for it. I struggled with it quite a bit when I just became an undead," Leonis replied.

He hadn't been especially proficient with sorcery during his time as a hero. And when he was first reborn as the Undead King by Roselia's power, he had too much mana and simply wielded it for indiscriminate destruction.

"Lady Riselia's greatest talents lie outside my field of expertise, so once she learns sorcery to an extent, it would be for the best for you to oversee her tutelage, my lord," Nefisgal stated.

Leonis nodded again. "True."

However, most of the magic Leonis knew was from the Realm of Death. The spells possessed eerie, ostentatious incantations, and Leonis imagined Riselia wouldn't be happy to use them.

"Then, my lord, I will be off..." With his duties concluded, Nefisgal made to return to the Realm of Shadows.

"Yes, good work."

Before the skeletal mage could leave, Riselia, who was lying on the ground, hurriedly stood.

"Th-thank you for all your guidance!" she called, bowing her head respectfully.

As rich young ladies went, Riselia had more sportsmanship than most.

"Good work today, Miss Selia," Leonis said as he approached and handed her a sports drink.

"Thanks, Leo," Riselia replied, taking a seat on the floor of the training room and downing the drink.

The sight of her supple legs in her sports outfit was quite tempting.

I'm not sure if an undead should look this healthy...

Leonis sat down next to his minion. "It looks like your sorcery training is progressing well," he remarked.

Riselia seemed doubtful. "I-it is?"

"Usually, it takes three years to learn how to handle mana and four more to pick up sorcery. By comparison, you're advancing very quickly."

"It feels kind of strange," Riselia admitted, gazing down at her hands. "Using mana like this..."

"For the time being, you're only capable of elementary magic," Leonis explained. "But since you're a Vampire Queen, you'll grow to cast sorcery of up to the seventh order."

"Order?"

"Spells are generally divided into orders. The higher one is, the more advanced its incantation becomes, and higher spells are stronger."

"What's the, um, highest order of spells you can cast, Leo?" Riselia asked.

"Me? Well... That's a secret." Leonis shook his head.

"Hmm..." Riselia stared at him fixedly and reached out with her hands.

"M-Miss Selia? Nng, h-hey, stop that...!"

Her cold fingertips tickled at his sides.

"...S-stop... Please stop that, Miss Selia! Fine, fine! The ninth order, I can cast spells up to the ninth order!" Left with no alternative, Leonis confessed.

Riselia ceased her relentless attack. "The ninth order?"

"...Yes. The ninth order is the greatest rank of sorcery," Leonis responded as he straightened his ruffled uniform. "Anything beyond exceeds the realm of sorcery, reaching the rank of a natural cataclysm or the like. Some even call them miracles. And in case you were wondering, Nefisgal can only cast spells up to the seventh order, too."

"Wow, Leo, you're really skilled, then," Riselia replied, her eyes wide with surprise.

I'm not a skilled sorcerer, I'm an all-powerful Dark Lord.

Unsurprisingly, Leonis had lied to Riselia. He could manage magic as powerful as the thirteenth order. His reincarnation spell was a twelfth-order spell, for example.

He kept magic above the tenth order reserved as a last resort against the Six Heroes or the Luminous Powers, however. Even the Undead King couldn't weave that kind of sorcery with ease. Worse, with this child's body, he likely wouldn't be able to withstand the cost that came with using such incredible magic.

"One does not learn sorcery in a day. It takes consistent practice," Leonis stated.

"Yes, understood," Riselia answered diligently before taking another swig of her sports drink.

"By the way, Miss Selia...," Leonis began.

"...Yes?"

"Would you mind if I got revenge for tickling me?"

Riselia considered her answer, placing a finger on her lips in a pensive gesture.

"Okay, Leo. Do you want to try to tickle me?"

"I was...joking," Leonis said, his cheeks reddening. A teasing smile spread on Riselia's face.

It feels like I can't win against her for some reason.

"Ah..." Riselia spread her arms out and then paused, her expression hardening for some reason.

"Is something wrong?" Leonis inquired.

"Y-yes... Well..." Riselia brought her hands to her chest. "Leo... Do you remember the day of the Holy Light Festival...?"

Seeing her grave expression, Leonis sensed something was amiss and straightened up. The day Riselia was referring to was when the Dragon Lord Veira awakened in the underground Void laboratory and went on a rampage.

Leonis had pursued Veira, leaving Riselia behind. She had met up with Arle and Sakuya, and the three girls squared off against Nefakess. Although the Void Lord lost his right arm in the battle and was forced to retreat...

"Did something happen back then?"

"...Y-yes," Riselia conceded and, after pausing to gather some courage, parted her lips again.

◆

"That's terribly important! Why didn't you tell me sooner?!" Leonis cried.

"I-I'm sorry! I just didn't want to worry you before an important mission...," Riselia replied, bowing apologetically.

While Veira had been rampaging over the Sixth Assault Garden, Riselia had fought Nefakess. During the struggle, he'd put some kind of black crystal into her chest.

"That could be terribly dangerous. Skilled sorcerers embed cursed tools into their opponents' bodies. They can even use them to control others like puppets." Leonis placed his hands on his waist and sighed. "You really should have been more careful... So do you feel different in any way?"

"My mana seems fine, and I can use my Holy Sword without a problem."

Hmm... Then this isn't a type of cursed tool that saps mana.

Leonis took a knee.

"Miss Selia, please lie down here."

"Huh?"

"Hurry," he urged her.

"A-all right...," Riselia said. Although visibly confused, she did as requested.

"This might hurt a little, but bear with it."

"H-huh?"

Her fair, toned limbs were covered in a set of two-piece training wear. With a serious expression, Leonis placed his palm over her chest.

"Leo?! Nng... Hii, mmm... ♪" Riselia writhed in place ticklishly.

"Stay still. And abstain from making weird noises..."

"Nng..." Riselia bit her lip and tried to stifle her breaths.

Her breasts, covered by her sports bra, rose and fell stiffly. Leonis closed his eyes, letting mana course through his fingers. By touching near Riselia's heart, he could peer into the mana flow of her entire body.

In humans, magic power typically gathered at the meridians, but for a Vampire Queen like Riselia, it circulated throughout her whole body.

There's something near her heart.

Leonis strained his closed eyes, and then...he saw it. A vaguely triangular crystalline object was embedded into her heart like a wedge.

Isn't that—?! He'd seen something very similar to this recently. *Isn't that the black crystal Zemein had?!*

Leonis had taken the object from Zemein's remains, but it hadn't exhibited any mana.

What does this mean? Why would Nefakess implant this in Riselia...?

"Nhahhh, L-Leooo...," Riselia groaned, her expression agonized.

"I'm sorry. Does it hurt?" Leonis asked her.

"Mmm... A little... But I'm fine..."

Evidently, Leonis's mana stimulated the crystal digging into her heart.

Extracting it would be dangerous.

The object had already partially fused with Riselia's body, and removing it would cause her terrible pain.

"Bear with it just a little longer. It'll be over soon."

"...All right."

Leonis held Riselia's hand with his free one. He focused on a point over her heart and channeled destructive magical power.

"Nngha?!"

Riselia's body thrashed, her back arching, and at that very moment, the crystal digging into her heart shattered to bits. Leonis gently released his minion's hand and wiped the cold sweat from his forehead.

It may have looked easy when Leonis did it, but destroying that crystal without damaging Riselia's body would have been an impossible task for the average sorcerer. Nefakess had surely never anticipated there'd be someone capable of removing it.

"You should be fine now. I crushed the crystal."

"Th-thank you...Leo," Riselia breathed, all the tension draining from her muscles.

Leonis checked her mana one more time, just in case, but all traces of the object were gone.

Still...

Leonis gritted his teeth. Nefakess Reizaad, that bishop. Why had he planted the crystal inside Riselia? Perhaps he'd set his sights on Riselia after the encounter in the Third Assault Garden.

Well, either way...

Leonis sneered devilishly. It wouldn't be long before that little upstart learned the true terror of a Dark Lord.

Forgiving though I may be, I have no mercy for those who lay hands on my minions.

A shrill alarm sounded, marking the end of their break time.

"Let's get going. Sakuya booked the next time slot," Leonis said, reaching out to Riselia and pulling her to her feet.

The indoor training facility needed to be reserved in advance, and the eighteenth platoon had booked it for today. Regina and Elfiné couldn't use the room due to their Holy Swords' properties, so Riselia, Leonis, and Sakuya took shifts.

"I think Sakuya opted out today," Riselia pointed out.

"Really?"

Sakuya might skip lectures, but she wasn't the sort to miss an independent training session.

"Yes, she said she'll be away from the dorms for a while because of the festival..."

"Festival?"

"Oh, right, you wouldn't know... Well, there's a self-governing section of Old Town. And every year, they have a traditional, religious enshrinement ritual."

Each Assault Garden was divided into relocation sectors meant to accommodate refugees from places destroyed by the Voids. Old Town, a part of the Seventh Assault Garden's second sector, was one such place. It was modeled after the Sakura Orchid's cities.

The sixth sector's biotope area, which was home to many demi-humans and beastmen, was another example of an area built for those displaced by Void destruction.

"Sakuya is a shrine maiden there, so each year she performs an offering dance to the Sakura Orchid's guardian deities."

"Sakuya is a shrine maiden?! Really?"

"Yes... Although I admit that I'm not very familiar with the Sakura Orchid's traditions."

Th-that's a surprise...

Something else piqued Leonis's curiosity, however.

"You said deities... Does the Sakura Orchid have gods?"

In Leonis's time, the deities were the Luminous Powers, who had declared themselves creators of this world, and the Goddess of Rebellion, who rose up against them.

There were also the demi-gods who served the Luminous Powers, and Demon Gods. One such Demon God was currently slumbering in Leonis's Realm of Shadows.

And I'd rather not awaken them, if at all possible.

It did beg the question of whether the deities of the Sakura Orchid were related to the ones Leonis knew.

I thought the legends of the Dark Lords, Luminous Powers, and Six Heroes had been forgotten, but...

Traces had survived, like fairy tales of Dark Lords who sought to bring the world to ruin.

I might want to look into the Sakura Orchid's enshrinement ritual.

However, sending Shary there would only get him a detailed report of the festival's best sweets.

"Umm...Leo?" Riselia's head was lowered, and she spoke timidly.

"...?"

"Like I said, Sakuya won't be coming today, so we still have some time."

"Y-yeah..."

"Nnn... So...could we?" she asked, her cheeks turning rosy as she grabbed Leonis's sleeve.

"Just a bit," he replied. "I still have classes during the afternoon."

"R-right. Just a bit."

Leonis had learned to pick up on the meaning behind Riselia's subtlest gestures. She had likely depleted much of her mana during this training session and was feeling fatigued.

Leonis offered his fingertip to her, and Riselia nibbled on it wantonly. A sweet numbness ran through the digit.

I really do become softhearted whenever my minions are involved, the Undead King mused self-deprecatingly.

◆

"Your Highness, the origin of that military vessel's freight is still unclear."

"I see... Thank you, Eika."

In Old Town, a short distance away from the bustling storefronts of Fuurin Street, stood a vast estate. Sitting in its courtyard was Sakuya, practicing her sword swings as she replied to the girl kneeling next to her.

This estate belonged to Raiou, the retainer to the Sakura Orchid's former royal house and Sakuya's legal guardian. In preparation for the enshrinement ritual that would take place four days from now, Sakuya had been visiting frequently over the last few days.

"Your Highness, please don't overexert yourself."

Sakuya shrugged and looked over her shoulder. "Yes, I know."

The girl behind her looked up at her with a slightly displeased expression. Eika was an operative of the Murakumo, a secret intelligence organization working for the royal house. Sakuya had asked Eika to investigate the Void appearance at the pier and the unidentified figure that called themselves a Dark Lord.

"I never imagined I'd run into the Voids there."

Last night, Sakuya had scouted out the Seventh Assault Garden, trying to detect any Demon Sword users after the recent appearance of several.

Demon Swords were the inverse of Holy Swords, which were a power granted by the planet. During a Hive Extermination mission a few days ago, three of Sakuya's upperclassmen, including Liat, were contaminated by Demon Swords and went berserk.

And it didn't end there. While it hadn't been made public information, multiple Holy Sword users had been corrupted by Demon Swords in the last few months.

Sakuya was gathering the power of other Demon Swords. By feeding their power to her own Demon Sword, Yamichidori, she could take in their abilities. As a cost, or perhaps as a side effect, she could now sense the presence of Voids.

This was why Sakuya had rushed to the pier, where she'd encountered the elf girl.

Those were definitely Voids last night.

Yet they hadn't come out of tears in space like most of their kind did. Those monsters had emerged from freight containers.

An imperial warship smuggled Voids into the city, hidden in crates...?

It was baffling.

Maybe the army collected Void specimens for research purposes?

Sakuya had never heard of a successful attempt at capturing Voids. The army had snared a few weaker ones, but they all disappeared into cracks in space.

And then there was the matter of the masked figure who had appeared in the middle of the battle...

"What about the so-called Dark Lord?" Sakuya asked the Murakumo operative.

"My apologies. I ordered Kuroyuki and Reigetsu to look into it, but they've yet to turn up anything."

"Don't worry, it's fine. I doubt it'd be easy to catch that figure."

"However...," Eika continued, looking up. "I'm not sure if there's any direct correlation, but there's been a change in the demi-human anti-imperial organizations' activities over the last couple of weeks."

"The terrorist cell that branched off from the capital's extremist group?"

Some time ago, insurgents called the Sovereign Wolves had hijacked the imperial royal family's ship, the *Hyperion*. However, a group of Holy Swordsmen on board (including Sakuya) interfered with their plan. Their leader, Bastea Colossuf, died in the incident, and the Sovereign Wolves were scattered.

Recently, it seemed they had gathered under someone else, who had rallied them once again.

"And you think this new leader of theirs is this so-called Dark Lord controlling the Seventh Assault Garden from the shadows?"

"Yes. It's only conjecture, but..."

"I see," Sakuya said, placing a finger on her pale lips as she recalled the Dark Lord's visage.

Massive Voids of A rank required a platoon-sized force to eliminate, and this Dark Lord had done so on his own. His power was overwhelming. Such strength was only possible with a Holy Sword...or a Demon Sword. Regardless, why would anyone with that level of might waste their time leading petty terrorists...?

But just then, the birdsong in the courtyard stopped.

"...?!"

Sakuya wheeled around as a heavy presence manifested in the nearby thicket.

"Who's there?!" Eika demanded, drawing a dagger from her sleeve and throwing it at the intruder.

The knife scattered a few leaves but didn't find purchase.

"The Murakumo is a far cry from its glory days." A voice spoke from atop a maple tree. "To think you'd allow me to enter this estate. Shameful."

Standing on a branch was a tall figure completely covered in black armor.

...Is that an anti-Void protect suit?!

Sakuya glared at the figure, her hand reaching for the grip of her katana.

"You...!" Eika growled at the figure as she reached into her sleeve to hurl another knife.

"Eika, wait." Sakuya stopped her.

"Your Highness...?"

Calmly, Sakuya questioned, "You're from the Kenki Gathering, aren't you?"

"Indeed, Princess Sakuya," a mechanically modified voice replied as the helmet's eyes glowed red.

"The Kenki Gathering?!" Eika raised her voice in surprise. "But why would you come here...?!"

The Kenki Gathering was an armed group that had served the Sakura Orchid's royal family for two centuries. While the Murakumo mainly was in charge of intelligence and espionage, the Kenki Gathering were the guards proper.

After the Sakura Orchid was destroyed by the Voids nine years ago, the Kenki Gathering became a group of wandering mercenaries seeking revenge for their fallen homeland. They traveled the world, fighting and slaying Voids wherever they could.

People would often liken Holy Swordsmen from the Sakura Orchid to berserkers, a comparison based on the Sakura Orchid's traditional combat style, which paid no heed to the fear of death.

"What did you come here for?!" Eika demanded. "You already parted ways with the royal family!"

"I came to warn you," the voice replied briefly. "The Voids approach. The Seventh Assault Garden will become a battlefield."

"What?" Sakuya was bewildered for a moment, and then her eyes widened in realization. "Don't tell me you were the ones who smuggled the Voids into the city?"

The figure did not answer. Whether that was denial or affirmation, none could say.

"Answer me. Depending on what you say, I might not allow you to leave this place," Sakuya declared, allowing a surge of electricity to run over Raikirimaru's blade.

"As the orphaned child of the royal house, we wish for you to take part in this fight, Princess Sakuya," the figure replied.

"Join your battle? Explain yourself..."

"I am only here to report our return to you, Princess Sakuya. I cannot reveal our plans here, with these bothersome flies buzzing about." The man in the protector suit laughed with a shrill voice. "I will speak to you again when you are alone, Princess Sakuya."

The figure then leaped away from the tree and faded like a shadow in the dark.

"Wait!" Eika made to go after him, but he was already gone.

This was a member of the Kenki Gathering, after all. He must have had an escape route planned well ahead of time.

"The Seventh Assault Garden will become a battlefield...?" Sakuya whispered the figure's words again and bit her lip.

Voids are coming. That much is clear.

Undoubtedly, this was related to the Void attack on the pier.

I have to stop this from happening...

The Kenki Gathering—a group of demons, possessed by a maddened urge for vengeance toward the Voids. They were going to bring something terrible upon this city.

But what do I do...?!

And as that urgent question filled her heart, *a particular image* flashed in Sakuya's mind.

◆

The Seventh Assault Garden had a massive, uninhabited float attached to the fourth industrial area. While the enormous city supported over one million people, a fourth of it was still undeveloped compared to the scale planned initially for the Assault Garden project. At one point, this section of the fourth industrial area was going to be an urban zone, and it still had many laminated structures.

Gathered in an underground space beneath those structures were some forty silhouettes. They were a very unusual group, for all of them were wearing anti-Void suits. One was speaking to someone through a communicator.

"That's right. The cargo you sent us is all gone."

"This won't get in the way of completing the plan, right?" another figure inquired.

"Those were just sent as an experiment," an encrypted voice answered through the communicator. **"You people are the crux of this plan."**

"We're grateful for your help, but we don't need those things," Uzan, the leader of the Kenki Gathering, said bitterly.

The man was regarded as the strongest Holy Swordsman in the Sakura Orchid.

But that's a thing of the past now. He scowled unpleasantly beneath his helmet.

To take revenge on the Voids that had ruined his homeland, he'd thrown himself into combat. He'd sacrificed everything to slay his nemesis—that Void Lord.

And now he was on the cusp of making that wish come true.

"Lord Phillet, we will do as we please from now on."

"Of course, go ahead. This is your revenge, after all," the voice on the other side of the transmission replied with a laugh.

Uzan's comrades—the Kenki Gathering—totaled thirty-seven members. Each was resolved to make a sacrifice that would claim their own lives and those of the Seventh Assault Garden's civilians.

And when our long-awaited wish comes true, we will all surely fall to hell.

In ninety-eight hours' time, a Stampede would destroy the city. That future was already set in stone.

Hopefully, Princess Sakuya will agree to join our side...

But then, abruptly, the sounds of footsteps could be heard echoing through the abandoned building.

"...?!"

In response, the members of the Kenki Gathering all kneeled as one, including Uzan. The sounds of the approaching figure were the only thing that disturbed the gloomy silence. A young woman approached, clad in a pure white outfit. Her long, waist-length blue hair wavered with each step.

"Princess Setsura…!"

"The time has come," the girl stated, her voice as clear as the chiming of a bell. "The Kenki Gathering will strike down our sworn foe—Shardark Void Lord."

The Kenki Gathering raised their voices in a war cry.

CHAPTER 3
TESSERA'S BIRTHDAY PARTY

"Yes, as previously discussed, there are many types of Holy Swords—"

"Phew..."

Leonis stifled a yawn, ignoring the teacher's lecture. Excalibur Academy allowed a student to put together and select their curriculum freely. However, Riselia had assembled Leonis's curriculum, and he didn't find the lectures terribly interesting. After all, it wasn't like he could use a Holy Sword himself.

Perhaps I've been overexerting myself.

Resting his chin on his desk, Leonis rubbed his sleepy eyes. There was that unexpected accident the night prior, and that morning he not only watched over Riselia's training but also had his blood sucked. As such, he was feeling a bit anemic at the moment.

He never needed to sleep when he was the Undead King, but his now ten-year-old body required quality slumber.

How incorrigible.

As he held back another yawn...

"Leo, are you all right?" Riselia, who occupied the seat next to him, asked worriedly.

"Are you sleepy, kid?" Regina teased. "You could always use my chest as a pillow if you want."

"N-no, I'm fine!" Leonis shook his head in a hurry. "How would I even do that? Do you mean a lap pillow?" Leonis asked wearily.

"Oh, I'm sure a breast pillow will be much nicer." Regina smirked.

She pressed her chest against Leonis's shoulder. It wasn't clear how serious she was.

"M-Miss Regina?!" Leonis squeaked out, his face red.

"Listen to the lecture, you two," Riselia whispered at them, honor student to the last.

Leonis fixed his eyes on the teacher again.

"The period in which a Holy Sword manifests changes by the individual, but regardless of gender, it manifests at five years of age at the earliest and twelve on average. There are exceptions, of course…"

Leonis got the feeling that the teacher had just snuck a glance at Riselia. She only manifested her Holy Sword at the age of fifteen, making her a late bloomer.

Holy Swords. The power the planet granted humankind.

These unusual weapons hadn't existed during Leonis's time. They had first manifested sixty-four years ago, during the first Void attacks. Holy Swords came in assorted forms that ranged from swords and bows to unusual things that humanity had never seen before. Holy Swords also seemed to mature with their wielders' souls. Similarly, they could lose their power if their owner experienced something traumatic.

Indeed, Elfiné lost the Eye of the Witch's original abilities for a long while.

And then there were Demon Swords.

If Holy Swords are the power of the planet, where do Demon Swords get their strength…?

Were the Holy Swords genuinely the might of the world? Leonis, continuing to ignore the lecture, could only wonder.

"Hey, Leo...," Riselia whispered into his ear.

"...?" Leonis directed his gaze at her.

"Aren't you almost at the age to manifest a Holy Sword yourself?"

"Huh?" Leonis was taken aback by the question.

"I mean, you're ten years old, and you keep fighting the Voids head-on. It makes sense the planet would grant you one soon."

"...I hadn't considered that."

Only humans could awaken to the power of Holy Swords. Beastmen and other demi-humans couldn't. A Dark Lord like Leonis shouldn't have been eligible. Or at least, that was what he'd assumed.

I do have the body of a human boy right now...

This form was that of Leonis Shealto, the Hero of the Holy Sword. In other words, he could potentially wield that power as well. But if that were the case, what would his Holy Sword look like? Supposedly, they were the materialization of one's soul. In which case...

A staff? Perhaps a sword? Or maybe a reaper's scythe?

After toying with that thought, Leonis shook his head silently.

I suppose it is a possibility, but...

His body might be human, but a Dark Lord who opposed humankind couldn't wield a Holy Sword. And as he came to that conclusion, the bell rang, marking the end of the lecture.

"Leo, we're going to Phrenia's for lunch today," Riselia said as she put her terminal into her bag.

"To the orphanage?"

Riselia helped out at Phrenia's orphanage, which doubled as an eatery.

"Tessera is celebrating her birthday today."

"Oh, is it?"

The eight-year-old Tessera was the most responsible girl in the orphanage. She'd grown quite attached to Leonis after witnessing him defend her home during a Stampede.

"That's no good, kid. You can't forget a girl's birthday." Regina raised a finger to scold him.

"Do you want to come with us, Leo? There's cake," Riselia said.

"Well... Yes, why not?"

There was merit to interacting with the orphanage's children. It was perfect for reaffirming his cover. No one would expect a ten-year-old child playing pretend with his fellow children to actually be the Dark Lord controlling this city from the shadows, after all.

Leonis nodded to himself in sinister approval.

◆

"A clash on the pier with an anti-imperial terrorist organization, eh...?"

Elfiné skimmed over the news as she partook of a late breakfast in her room in the dormitory.

"Seems as if a lot of things like that have been happening recently."

When the Assault Garden Project came to be, many of the demi-human nations were basically forced to join the Integrated Human Empire. The discontent that caused hadn't yet faded entirely.

Elfiné took a bite of her buttered toast and sipped her coffee. Being an honors student, she'd already attended most of her lectures. Thus she had no classes for the first half of the day, making her morning quite leisurely.

However, since scanner-type Holy Swords were rare, they were often called upon to help companies tackle various problems that cropped up in the city. And the most recent such matter was the enshrinement ritual festival set to take place in the Sakura Orchid self-governed area in a few days.

I accepted the job willingly, so I can't complain about the extra work.

A few days ago, Liat, a member of the Executive Committee, had been corrupted by a Demon Sword and lost his abilities as a Holy Swordsman. Elfiné had wound up taking up his share of the Executive Committee's work.

Elfiné couldn't let whoever did that to Liat get away unpunished. And her only clues as to who that might be were the existence of the elusive Demon Sword Project, the voice of a goddess that Muselle and other students affected by Demon Swords reported hearing, and an Artificial Elemental called Seraphim.

The Phillet Company had produced Seraphim, and while it was currently unavailable for purchase, it seemed that a Demon Sword would take hold of those led by its voice.

The capital's Demon Sword Project... Father has to be involved.

Glaring down at her terminal, Elfiné bit her lip as her black locks covered her eyes.

"Finé. ♪"

"Aaaah!"

Feeling a pair of arms embrace her from behind, Elfiné shook, nearly spilling coffee all over her terminal.

"C-C-Clauvia?!" she squeaked, whirling around.

Sure enough, her older sister was there.

"H-how did you get in here?!" Elfiné demanded, rattled.

"How? Well, through the door," her sister replied, casually jabbing her thumb in the direction of the entrance.

Clauvia's Holy Sword allowed her to conceal her presence from others. If she put her mind to it, even Elfiné's fully powered Eye of the Witch couldn't locate her.

"That's not what I meant," Elfiné grumbled, massaging her temples nervously. "What are you here for? If you're hoping to convince me to help you in the capital, I already said no."

"You're so cold. I just came to check on my baby sister."

"..."

Clauvia had to be scheming at more than just that.

There's no way she's here for something so innocent.

Clauvia then looked down at Elfiné's terminal and raised an eyebrow. Apparently, she was interested in the report about the terrorist attack on the pier.

"Very unpleasant news," she commented.

"Unpleasant?"

An anti-imperial faction attack wasn't too unusual.

"Pressure from the military kept the press from reporting what actually happened."

"Censorship? But why—"

Elfiné's older sister was a leading technological officer in the Phillet Company, with connections in places as high as the palace. Her being privy to confidential intelligence wasn't odd. And anything she couldn't learn from her informants, she discovered by hacking the Astral Garden.

"Apparently, a battle against Voids broke out."

"Voids?" Elfiné's eyes widened.

If Voids appeared in the city, Excalibur Academy's central administration bureau should have contacted local intelligence officers, including Elfiné.

Elfiné rested a hand on her chin. "So the military kept it quiet. It didn't happen in an urban area, so I guess they're hoping to prevent any unnecessary concern. Still, they should have reported it to Excalibur Academy…"

"Right? That got me curious, too. So I looked into it, and…" Clauvia paused, bringing her lips to Elfiné's ear. "Some of the freight on the ship that docked that night came from Finzel's enterprise."

"…?!"

Finzel Phillet. The Phillet family's second elder son, and one of their father's heirs. He was among the people listed as involved in the capital's Demon Sword Project…

"Don't tell me the Void attack is related somehow…"

"Honestly, I don't know the answer to that," Clauvia replied with a shrug. "But brother dearest has been acting suspicious lately."

"What makes you say that?"

"Apparently, he contracted a mercenary group of Sakura Orchid survivors to handle his personal security."

"Sakura Orchid mercenaries…? You mean the Kenki Gathering?"

"Oh, you've heard of them?"

"I have. One of my teammates is from the Sakura Orchid."

The Kenki Gathering was an armed group devoted to hunting down Voids. Its members were seasoned Holy Swordsmen and survivors of the Sakura Orchid Stampede.

"Don't you think hiring them for his private army seems a bit overblown?" Clauvia asked suggestively.

"…Yes, it does."

If Clauvia was telling the truth, Elfiné had to wonder what their brother hoped to achieve. Maybe this was the will of that monster from the capital—their father.

"Either way, you should watch out for Finzel. Think of this as a bit of cordial advice from your big sister. ♪"

"..."

"I'll be returning to the emperor's brother soon. Do consider my work proposal, though," Clauvia said and, with that comment, left the room.

◆

The city seems quite peaceful, despite what happened yesterday.

The elven hero, Arle Kirlesio, walked along the edge of the road, looking around with a hood pulled low over her face. The laminated buildings around her were taller than her forest's trees. There was only one place in this city where a girl like her, who grew up in nature's embrace, could feel at home: the artificial biotope populated by the demi-humans.

And despite that, she had to visit the more urban areas to purchase daily necessities that were hard to procure in the biotope.

I need some new clothes. And one of those magical devices everyone seems to be using might be nice.

Arle was dressed in child's clothes she'd found in the remnants of the Third Assault Garden. Her physique was slender and small enough for them to fit her perfectly, but she still wanted something slightly more presentable.

She also wanted one of the magical apparatuses people in this age used to gather intelligence. Lena had given Arle a forged citizen's permit, so she should be able to acquire one with no issue.

Lena had offered to accompany her on her shopping trip, but Arle had refused. She may have been hiding among the Demon Wolf Pack, but that was only to investigate and eventually assassinate the Dark Lord Zol Vadis.

Getting too close to them would just make me waver when it matters most.

Arle's display during the incident last night had earned her some degree of trust in the group. The day when she would be promoted into the Dark Lord's inner circle wasn't far off.

I will defeat the resurrected Dark Lord. That is my mission...

Unconsciously, Arle's fingers gripped the hilt of the Demon Smiting Sword Crozax, which was hidden under her cloak. Zol Vadis had effortlessly destroyed the Voids on the pier. If Arle were to challenge him directly, she'd almost certainly fail.

I'm not sure if that really is the Zol Vadis I know of, though.

Arle had never met the Zol Vadis of one thousand years ago. Her fellow apprentice and brother figure, Leonis, had felled that Dark Lord. However, he later became the strongest and most terrible of all Dark Lords—the Undead King.

And there's no guarantee only one Dark Lord has returned.

If more appeared, there might come a time when she had to battle the Undead King.

But then...

"...P-please, stop it!"

"You're just losers! If Leo was here—ah!"

She could hear the voices of small children crying out from an alleyway.

"Huh? That brat just smeared mud all over my clothes!"

Arle's ears twitched as they caught the gruff voice of an adult man.

I shouldn't poke my head into trouble if I can avoid it...

Still, Arle was a hero, and she couldn't ignore injustice. She made for the side street where the commotion was coming from. There she found three children cowering in fear, cornered by a pair of young men.

"Stop this," Arle commanded. "Threatening children? Have you no shame?"

"Huh?! Who're you?!" the ruffians shouted, turning to face the elf girl. "Do you know what these refugee kids did to us?!"

"I see that no matter how far magic technology has advanced, there are still some people who can't understand basic speech." Arle quietly began an incantation. "Deig Ray."

""Gaaaaaaah!""

Arle fired a small jolt of electricity from her fingers, knocking the men out in an instant. She made sure to restrain the spell's power, so they weren't dead.

Looking to the children, she said, "Go on, leave. And be careful this time."

"Y-yes... Thank you!" The oldest girl of the trio bowed her head thankfully.

Upon seeing her face, Arle's blue eyes widened in realization. She knew this child. When she had nearly passed out from hunger some time ago, this girl had aided her.

And just as Arle recalled who she was, the girl seemingly recognized the elf, too, despite the hood.

"You're that lady...right?"

"...Aaah, erm..." Arle awkwardly averted her gaze.

It was embarrassing to be reminded of nearly collapsing from starvation.

"U-um..." The girl approached and bashfully pinched the hem of Arle's mantle. "I'd like to thank you for saving us. You can come to our orphanage if you'd like..."

"I-it's fine. I don't require any gratitude." Arle shook her head. Modesty was a heroic virtue, after all.

However...

"It's Tessera's birthday party today!"

"Riselia and her friends are gonna come and make lots of yummy food and cake!"

The other two kids, a lively girl and a bespectacled boy, were insistent.

C-cake...?

That sort of food didn't exist in the forest where Arle grew up. When Arle first tasted cake in this city, she'd been so overwhelmed with emotion that she'd forgotten Crozax in the bakery.

"Cake...," Arle muttered wistfully.

Since she was broke most of the time, sweets were an indulgence beyond Arle's reach.

"Regina's cake is so tasty. It puts a smile on your face. ♪"

"A smile..." Arle repeated the words, absolutely salivating.

She needed to shop for necessities and one of those magical devices, but she was in no rush to do so.

"A-are you too busy to come with us?" the older girl asked, looking up at her with eyes like a fawn's.

"I—I could come for a little while," Arle replied, twirling the end of her ponytail with a finger.

◆

That afternoon, Riselia, Regina, and Leonis headed to Phrenia's orphanage after shopping for ingredients in the city center.

"Phew, this should be enough," Riselia remarked as she loaded the wooden crate from their military vehicle.

"You did buy quite the stock," Leonis commented.

"Well, it's for all the kids. If we've got anything leftover, we'll just take it back to the dorms."

"I-it is kind of heavy...," Regina said as she struggled to pick up a bag of ingredients.

"Let me carry it for you, Regina," Leonis proposed.

"Huh? You sure you can handle it, kid?" Regina eyed him dubiously.

"...I do keep up with my basic training, you know," Leonis asserted, easily lifting a hefty sack.

"Wow... You really are a boy, aren't you?" Regina whispered in surprise.

"Are you cheating, Leo?" Riselia asked with a little smile.

"You can tell, huh?"

Leonis had used a gravity spell to lighten the bag's weight. Riselia had noticed because of her sorcery training.

"Were you testing me to see if I would notice the spell?" she whispered.

"Something like that."

"Hm, what are you two muttering about?" Regina asked, looking a bit perplexed.

As they neared the orphanage, the children playing outside noticed and hurried over.

"They're here!"

"Selia!"

"Leo's here!"

"Ah, Regina!"

"Regina came!"

"Leoooo!"

"Hmm, why am I the only one without a nickname?" Regina grumbled.

"Regina, hurry up with the cake!"

"Yes, yes, of course... Hey, don't tug on my hair!"

A couple of playful boys started toying with Regina's pigtails.

"You're very popular with the children, Regina."

"Hahhh... If only they were as mature as you, kid," Regina said with a sigh as the children kept toying with her hair.

◆

"Thank you for taking the time to visit. The kitchen is this way."

Having heard their voices, the orphanage's owner, Phrenia, came out to guide Leonis, Riselia, and Regina. However, when Phrenia opened the door to the kitchen...

"...?!"

Leonis spotted a girl sitting at a table. He was so stunned that he very nearly dropped the bag he was carrying.

What?!

The girl who was staring at him stiffly was none other than—

Why is Arle Kirlesio here?!

There was no mistaking her. It was the same hero he'd seen last night.

"Y-you!" Regina pointed fixedly at the girl. "Aren't you that elf girl we picked up in the Third Assault Garden?!"

"N-no, I think you have the wrong elf...!" Arle responded, pulling the hood over her head in a flustered manner.

It was too late, though. Regina had recognized her.

"Where did you run off to?" Riselia questioned. "We didn't have time to finish your citizen registration."

When they'd all returned from the ruined city in a tactical fighter, Arle had disappeared as soon as they'd landed in the Seventh Assault Garden. After that, she'd joined the Demon Wolf Pack, although Leonis was the only one besides the elf who knew that.

"..." Arle held her tongue, hood still pulled over her face.

"Hm, are you...friends already?" Tessera, who was seated next to the hero, asked sheepishly. "Miss Arle just helped us—"

"I think I'll be leaving," Arle interjected, getting to her feet. "Thank you."

"W-wait!" Tessera hurriedly grabbed her by the arm.

"If you have problems of some sort, we won't force you to join Excalibur Academy," Riselia explained. "You helped us back in the ruined city, after all."

"..."

"Besides, since you're here, you should at least have some cake." Tessera nodded. "Y-yes, that's a good idea!"

"V-very well," Arle said, reluctantly settling back into her seat.

◆

Pop, pop, pop, pop!

Party crackers sounded.

"Happy ninth birthday, Tessera!"

"Th-thank you! Thank you so much!" Tessera bowed her head gratefully with a smile.

The dining room's table was full of present boxes. Riselia got Tessera a picture book she liked, and Regina got her stamping patterns for making cookies.

"I got you this..."

Leonis had brought a present, too. He took out a luxurious box containing...

"...!"

A small statue carved out of bone. Leonis had used remains he'd gathered from Necrozoa to piece together a tiny dragon.

"L-Leo...?" Riselia looked at him quizzically.

"Making this was backbreaking work," Leonis stated proudly, making a joke. "Thankfully, unlike mine, this one's spine is intact."

"It's so creepy!"

"Eew..."

"It looks like it might come to life at night!"

For some reason, the orphanage's children (especially the girls) didn't seem to like it very much.

"Your tastes might be a bit too refined for them, kid...," Regina said with a troubled expression.

"B-but you did work hard on it!" Riselia reassured him, although her face was just as uneasy as her maid's.

"It is very well made." Arle was the only one to offer genuine praise. "It looks like the real thing."

Wh-why can't they understand how impressive it is?! Leonis thought, upset by the less-than-warm reaction.

However...

"Th-thank you, Leo! I love it!" Tessera shouted as if to drown out all the others. "I mean, if you look at it close enough, it's kind of cute... I think!"

C-cute... Is it?

Leonis wasn't sure about the girl's appraisal, but she did seem happy to have it.

"Heh-heh, I guess you're more considerate than you look, kid ♪," Regina teasingly whispered into his ear.

"Oh, I know, we could put it up outside to ward off thieves," Phrenia suggested.

Nodding in approval, Leonis replied, "Yes, I think that's a good idea."

He'd put a second-order Animated Guardian spell on this

statuette. The magic would bring the little dragon to life to defend the building in case something happened.

"It's time, everyone. Enjoy the cake!" Regina called. The children cheered as she stood and got to work.

Arle cheered alongside them before suddenly realizing what she was doing and bashfully stopping herself.

◆

While Regina and Riselia were handling the cooking, Leonis was told to play with the children in the living room.

What...should I be doing exactly?

Leonis glared enviously at Riselia, who stood in the kitchen. Tessera was the oldest girl in the orphanage, with the siblings Millet and Linze tied for second. Thus, it often fell to Tessera to look after the little ones.

I hardly have any memories of playing with children...

As he sat in a corner of the room, Leonis probed through his distant memories. Much like these kids, Leonis was an orphan. At the time, the Rognas Kingdom had been ravaged by war with a Dark Lord, leaving many without their parents. There were no places for displaced kids, so many had to survive as street urchins.

A man who had rescued a certain six-year-old boy from that terrible fate went on to become one of the Six Heroes. And Leonis followed suit, single-mindedly polishing his skills with the blade under that man's tutelage.

What a twist of fate it was that the same child later became a Dark Lord and enemy of the world.

Evidently, destiny hadn't given up on toying with Leonis's bond to his old teacher. He snuck a glance at the elf girl sitting wearily on the opposite side of the room. Arle Kirlesio had studied under the same master as Leonis, making her his sister apprentice.

She'd hardly known any contact with humans. The forest elves were a reclusive, fastidious people. Barring the most extreme circumstances, they'd never have willingly left their forest to interact with others.

This is quite the development, but it's a good chance nonetheless. Let's investigate her.

Leonis got to his feet and approached Arle.

She regarded him suspiciously. "Wh-what do you want...?"

"U-um, could you play with me?"

"H-huh?!" Her long ears twitched with surprise.

The words almost felt like a pickup line, but Leonis was currently a ten-year-old boy. This wasn't all that bizarre.

"Er, I'm sorry, I... I've never played with human children before."

"Oh, that's fine. You don't have to do anything. *I'll do the playing.*"

"...Huh?"

Leonis curled up his lips into a smirk and chanted.

"Third-order mind spell—Varis Ro Zelma."

The moment he'd finished chanting, the light faded from Arle's eyes. Although she had attempted to resist the magic, the elf was powerless before Leonis's sorcery.

Leonis casually took a seat next to Arle, pretending to be chatting with her so as not to arouse any suspicion from Tessera and the others.

Now, what should I ask her...?

"Were you sent to this era by the Elder Tree?" he inquired.

"...Yes. The Elder Tree...gave me a mission..."

"Hm. Yes, I assumed as much..."

The Elder Tree was part of the Holy Tree that grew in the heart of the world, and was a subordinate deity to the God of the Forest. The Archsage, Arakael Degradios, had fused with the Holy Tree, but the Elder Tree seemed to have survived.

"And your mission is to slay the Dark Lords that would revive in this era, right?"

Arle nodded, her face blank. "...Yes. I am to use Crozax to fell them."

"How did you plan on seeking out the Dark Lords?"

"That is simple. Wherever the Dark Lords go, ruin and chaos are sure to follow..."

"...Not necessarily," Leonis said, wearing a displeased expression.

However, it was a fair enough method to locate Veira, the Dragon Lord; Gazoth, the Lord of Beasts; and Dizolf, the Lord of Rage. Cautious Dark Lords who tried to conceal their presence, like Leonis, were the minority.

Evidently, Arle didn't know much more than Leonis did. He was a bit disappointed but continued his questioning.

"Do you have any information regarding the goddess—about Roselia Ishtaris's reincarnation?"

The change was sudden.

"...Lia... Rose...lia... Goddess... Void...st..."

What?!

Arle's eyes widened, and she started repeating words deliriously.

"God...dess...yet...come...two..."

Is this some kind of defensive reaction against my magic? But that shouldn't...

Leonis concentrated mana into his eyes and peered directly into Arle's mind. At that moment, an electric shock ran through his head.

Impossible! Something rebuked me...?!

It was a mind break curse. The soul of an average sorcerer

would have been severed instantly. Leonis could sense someone else watching behind Arle Kirlesio.

There's something observing me?

Leonis immediately undid the mind thrall and chanted a curse detection spell on himself to ensure he hadn't been ensorcelled. Thankfully, the attack had lasted for only a moment and wouldn't cause any long-term effects.

Who did that?

The first possible suspect was the Elder Tree that had sent Arle to this era. It might have been observing her actions through her eyes. However...

No. That wasn't the Elder Tree's presence. It was something else. Leonis was sure of that. *This was a failure. I shouldn't have made a move on her recklessly.*

Even if whoever was on the other side didn't identify Leonis specifically, his actions made it clear that someone had tried to dominate Arle's mind.

She reacted to Roselia's name... Or was it the word goddess*?*

"Mm... Nng, huh...?" The light returned to Arle's eyes. "What happened...?"

"It looks like you dozed off a bit. Are you tired?" Leonis inquired innocently.

"Eh? Hm, yes, a lot happened last night...," Arle replied, her mind clearly still a bit muddled.

The elf didn't seem to be aware that someone was observing her.

I should let her continue as she pleases until I figure out who this watcher is, Leonis concluded.

"Everyone, the food's ready!" Riselia called out from the kitchen.

◆

"Wow! ♪" Tessera's eyes sparkled as she beheld the table, which was now packed with dishes.

A chicken roast garnished with sweet berry sauce and freshly baked buns. Bacon and soup cooked with vegetables picked from Riselia's private garden. Pilaf with meatballs, stir-fried beans, pasta with cheese, meat gratin, baked clams taken from the aquaculture plant, peeled sweet corn. And last but not least, Regina's special demi-glace hamburg steaks, a favorite of Leonis's.

"I think we might have made too much, so you all better eat up!" Regina said with a wink as the kids pounced on the food, competing to see who could scarf down more.

"Y-you're forgetting your table manners...," Tessera protested meekly.

"You should eat, Tessera!" the others told her, too focused on consuming.

"Don't be shy. Help yourself, Leo," Riselia told him.

"Pardon, but I'm no child," Leonis replied in a dignified manner, despite already having a hamburg steak on his plate.

"Be sure to eat your veggies, too. See? Just like her," Riselia chided, motioning to Arle. The girl was silently chewing on some bread and greens at the edge of the table.

"She's an elf...," Leonis retorted with exasperation.

"It's like a festival in here," Phrenia remarked with a smile. Then she bowed to Riselia. "I can't express how grateful I am."

"Oh, not at all," Riselia said. "You help me out so much all the time."

Millet looked up, her cheeks dirty with sauce. "Hey, Leo! There's a Sakura Orchid Festival coming up!"

"Hm? Yes, so I've heard." It was just this morning that Riselia had told him about the upcoming event. "Will you be attending?"

"Yeah! And Tessera was wondering if you could come with—"

"M-Millet!" Tessera suddenly went very red and nearly choked.

"Why not go, kid?" Regina suggested, a small smile on her lips. "The rest of the platoon will be attending to watch Sakuya's dance."

"Yes, I suppose I should, then." Leonis accepted. He was interested in this Sakura Orchid ritual. He'd never visited the Sakura Orchid's sector himself, and most importantly, he wanted to know more about this ancient god they revered. "I think I'd like to go."

Tessera let out a small cheer at Leonis's confirmation. "Then let's all meet up tomorrow and go there."

"Understood."

Yet just as Leonis nodded, he received a telepathic message from Shary.

"—M-my lord, my lord! There's an emergency!"

"What's wrong, Shary?"

"There's an unidentified intruder in the Dark Lord's Castle!"

"...What?"

CHAPTER 4

 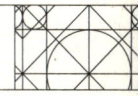

INTRUDER IN THE DARK LORD'S CASTLE

"*Someone...infiltrated the Dark Lord's Castle?*" Leonis repeated telepathically. "*What scoundrel would dare... How many of them are there?*"

"*Based on the beastmen's report, it's likely just one target. Details like their affiliation are unknown, but...,*" Shary answered.

Hmm, Leonis thought.

The Dark Lord's Castle's dungeon was accessible through a portal located deep beneath the Seventh Assault Garden. It wasn't an easy place to reach.

"*It seems the intruder took one of the beastmen hostage, and they guided the intruder to the gate.*"

So that's how.

Perhaps he should have been angrier at the beastman for his lack of loyalty, but he wasn't an undead soldier without self-preservation instincts.

This just proves I haven't gained complete control over my minions, that's all.

"What, kid, full already?" Regina looked at Leonis with visible concern, seeing he wasn't touching his food.

"No, I was just thinking, is all," Leonis replied, biting into the hamburg steak on his plate.

"*Do I have permission to exterminate the shameless intruder, my lord?*" Shary inquired.

"Hm, yes... Actually, no. I'm interested in this scoundrel." After pausing to consider, Leonis changed his mind. "*I'll go myself. Out of respect for the courage, no, the foolhardiness they exhibited by charging into the Dark Lord's Castle alone. I will bring them to their knees and have them serve me.*"

"*Then I am to let them continue unimpeded?*"

"Correct. But this is also a good chance to test the castle's defensive measures, so make sure to greet them courteously."

"*Understood, my lord...*"

Leonis wolfed down the remainder of his food and got to his feet.

"What's wrong, Leo?" Riselia asked.

"I think I might have overeaten. Which way to the restroom?"

After fabricating an excuse, Leonis hurried into the hall, where he summoned a bone warrior from his shadow.

"One of the Three Champions of Rognas, Hell's Grappler, Dorug, at your service," the skeleton said.

"I will be returning to my castle. I need you to act as my body double for the time being."

"Understood, my lord!"

With that, Leonis cast a shape-shifting spell on Dorug. The skeletal warrior's form distorted momentarily and then took on Leonis's visage.

"I'm counting on you. Just be sure not to do anything suspicious," Leonis instructed him before vanishing into the shadows.

◆

"I never imagined I'd find something like this under the city…"

As she slipped through the bright, shimmering portal, the intruder gasped in surprise. She found herself in a vast subterranean complex illuminated by many iron lanterns. A long stone corridor extended before her.

Something so large couldn't have existed below the Seventh Assault Garden. Thus, that gate must have been…

A teleportation device of some sort.

Even the capital didn't have that kind of magical technology, however.

"P-please, I showed you to the gate! Spare me…!" the beastman in her grip pleaded with a strained expression. Her blade was pressed against his neck.

"Not yet. Show me to your Dark Lord."

"I—I can't. Only the highest-ranking members of our group know where the Dark Lord resides. You could get to him if you reach the bottom of the labyrinth, but the way there is full of dangerous monste—"

"You talk too much, beastman. Are you going to lead me or not?" The intruder, Sakuya Sieglinde, mercilessly dug into the beastman's throat with the tip of her katana.

Even the Murakumo's intelligence gathering couldn't sniff out any helpful information regarding the Dark Lord's identity. Fortunately, they had successfully located the Demon Wolf Pack by tracking the scattered remaining members of the Sovereign Wolves. Sakuya had contacted one of them and was forcing him to take her to the Dark Lord.

"P-please, just let me go already!" the beastman begged.

"Sorry, but no. Believe me—I'd rather not stoop to this, either," Sakuya responded coldly.

The Dark Lord Zol Vadis. The one who ruled this city from behind the scenes.

If he really controls the Seventh Assault Garden, he definitely won't let the Kenki Gathering go through with their plan.

Sakuya was still unsure of the Kenki Gathering's machinations, but they had said the Seventh Assault Garden would become a battlefield. Sakuya was just like them, an avenger seeking to hunt down the Voids, but she would never accept a method that put innocents at risk.

At the same time, the young swordswoman was wise enough to understand that she couldn't stop a group hellbent on revenge by herself. She'd already submitted an anonymous report to Excalibur Academy's administration bureau, and ever since the *Hyperion*'s hijacking, the Seventh Assault Garden's anti-terrorist caution level had been elevated to the maximum.

But this means going up against the Kenki Gathering, the Sakura Orchid's elites. The administration bureau won't be able to handle them.

The Seventh Assault Garden was a frontline bastion in the fight against the Voids. However, unlike the capital, it lacked a special organization for dealing with internal terrorist activities.

With nowhere else to turn, Sakuya had sought out another faction in the city.

If I can just join forces with the Dark Lord...

The question was whether she'd be able to win his cooperation. It was definitely a gamble. If this so-called Dark Lord really saw the city as his domain, he had to feel compelled to rescue it from crisis. But if Sakuya's negotiations failed, she could very well meet her demise.

"Go on. Lead me to your Dark Lord."

"E-eek!"

Just as Sakuya made to dig her blade a little deeper into the beastman...

"I welcome you to my castle, brave yet foolish swordswoman."

"...?!"

A booming voice sounded through the labyrinth's corridors.

"You're the Dark Lord—Zol Vadis!"

"In honor of your reckless valor, I shall entertain you appropriately!"

Blue will-o'-the-wisps burst to life in the air, illuminating a path forward.

"You're...guiding me to you?"

"Indeed. But first, you must clear my trials. Only by conquering my labyrinth will you be allowed to reach my residence."

"Bring it on," Sakuya said, releasing her hostage and readying Raikirimaru. Electricity crackled over the weapon's blade.

This might be a trap...

Still, this was no time to hesitate. With her Holy Sword in hand, Sakuya sprinted off.

◆

How did Sakuya get here?!

Leonis massaged a temple with one hand while seated on his throne of bones. Reflected in the crystal ball he held in his other was a blue-haired girl. Her Sakura Orchid attire billowed as she sped forward. Leonis had suspected she might try to uncover the Dark Lord's identity, but...

This exceeds my every expectation. How did she manage to storm my castle after only a day...?

What did the young woman hope to accomplish? Surely Sakuya wasn't like one of those heroes a millennium ago that hoped to slay a Dark Lord.

"I suppose I'll just have to see what she's capable of..."

Leonis knew of Sakuya's skills from the training matches in

the academy. Her individual combat prowess was second to none, and though she appeared reckless at first sight, she possessed keen judgment skills. Her blade skills rivaled Leonis's before he'd become the Undead King.

And to top it all off, her Holy Sword, Raikirimaru, boosted the wielder's speed.

Leonis watched through his orb as Sakuya streaked past the skeleton soldiers, effortlessly cutting them down. She was already moving faster than an ordinary human's eyes could follow.

I'd like her as a minion.

In truth, Leonis's army was primarily formed of undead, but even with sufficient mana, he couldn't create them on end. He needed corpses, be it simple skeletons, ghouls, or skull dragons.

A thousand years ago, when war waged nonstop, he had a steady supply. Things weren't that simple in this era, though. The Voids, those mysterious life-forms, if they could even be called such, tended to vanish into the emptiness whence they came and couldn't be used for Leonis's magic.

While he now had the Demon Wolf Pack under his command, and their brute strength was remarkable, they still weren't experienced enough in combat. Given weapons and ample combat training, they might form a unit as mighty as the Dizolf Grand Beast's Demon Beast Corps. At present, however, they were a far cry from that potential.

But if I can enlist Sakuya into the Dark Lords' Armies...

"My lord." Shary appeared near Leonis's throne, kneeling before him respectfully while holding up a tray with a tea set. "I brought you something to drink."

"Thank you." Leonis nodded, took a cup, and sipped the tea.

Shary was altogether a ditz as maids went, but if there was one thing she was good at, it was serving tea.

"What do you think that swordswoman's objective might be?" Shary asked as she looked into Leonis's crystal ball.

"I don't know. But it surely isn't to join my ranks," he replied. Turning his attention to the shadow at his feet, he called, "Blackas, come join us. You're close with her, are you not?"

"We have some connection, yes." The darkness swelled, taking the shape of a large black wolf. "She's a proud girl with the heart of a true fighter."

"Hmm. What do you think about recruiting her into the Dark Lords' Armies?"

Blackas's ears twitched, and Shary raised an eyebrow slightly.

"I believe that is your decision to make as supreme commander of the Dark Lords' Armies," the great wolf answered softly.

"...I see," Leonis said before falling silent as he observed Sakuya's image on the orb.

Warriors as skilled as Sakuya Sieglinde were hard to come by. And since she was only fourteen years of age, she had room to grow. Riselia was capable as a frontline commander, but Sakuya was a mighty vanguard.

If Leonis was to compare Sakuya to any of his existing minions, she was most like the Underworld Knight Schteizer Halliorstatt, one of his most accomplished champions.

And besides...

"If I were to take in Sakuya, a member of her kingdom's royal family, I might be able to recruit all of the Sakura Orchid's people in one fell swoop—"

Of course, things weren't guaranteed to go that easily. Regardless, Leonis and Sakuya had a common enemy in the Voids. There was certainly enough grounds for them to join forces.

"Nnnnnn. My lord, are you plotting to blindly create more minions again?" Shary questioned, puffing her cheeks in displeasure.

"It seems she broke through the skeleton soldiers, Lord Magnus," Blackas reported, heedless of Shary's complaints.

"Impressive. But I expected no less," Leonis said, knowing that low-ranking bone warriors were no match for Sakuya. "Next, send out the Shadow Beasts."

◆

"Hyahhhhhhhh, Thundering Lightning Slash!"

Sakuya's blade danced through the air, cloaked in electricity, as it freely cut through the skeletons. Bones scattered into the air, hitting the labyrinth walls and breaking into dust.

These bone monsters... Is the Dark Lord creating them?

Individually, they weren't strong, but it was taxing to face them in large numbers.

"Having so much to slash is fun in its own way, though...!"

Shwing!

Her sword arced like a bolt of lightning as it swept through a whole company of shambling bones. It seemed she'd felled the last of them.

"Haah, haah, haah."

But just as Sakuya began to relax and steady her labored breathing...

Grrrrrrrrrroar!

The shadows cast by the flickering will-o'-the-wisps grew and came to life, becoming a Shadow Beast.

"...!"

Sakuya reflexively dodged and slashed at the creature. However, it wasn't over yet. The shadows seethed like boiling water, and more animal-like silhouettes rose.

"Shoot!"

Slashing through the monsters, Sakuya tried to push forward, but the Shadow Beasts had already cut ahead of her. Unlike the bone warriors, these creatures hunted their prey in a coordinated, organized manner.

I wish I could get a read on how many of them there are... And their attack patterns, Sakuya thought while evading incoming attacks.

She longed for Elfiné's analysis and Riselia's accurate command.

Miss Regina's covering fire would make things much easier...

And there was also the boy who'd recently joined their unit, Leonis. He hadn't made any particularly eye-opening achievements in combat yet, but just having him around seemed to help the unit function more smoothly.

Up until six months ago, coordination with her teammates never crossed Sakuya's mind. She had tried being part of a unit of upperclassmen, but always ended up hunting Voids solo. That was the only way she knew, and it eventually led to her dismissal from that squad.

That's how I've always fought.

A proud, aloof sword that swept through the Voids like a demon.

I don't think I'm weaker for fighting in a team, but the brand of strength I wield has changed, for sure.

The Shadow Beasts howled as they reached for Sakuya's limbs. She tried to slash at one holding her right leg, but more and more of its kin appeared, dragging her down into the dark.

The miasma of nothingness began to pour from Sakuya's body.

Crackle, crackle, crackle...!

Tendrils of black lightning licked Raikirimaru's blade. The Demon Sword Yamichidori. This was Sakuya's trump card against the Voids—one she had kept secret from her teammates. The surging bolts instantly destroyed the beasts pinning her, forcing them to melt into the shadows.

"Not at a...time like this...!"

Sakuya swung the blade's tip down, turning it from a Demon Sword back to Raikirimaru. Using the Demon Sword, even for a short moment, allowed the nothingness to eat away at her.

"The Dark Lord certainly has some powerful servants...," Sakuya remarked, her shoulders trembling as she breathed slowly while pushing deeper into the labyrinth.

"Oh, so you've overcome the Shadow Beasts. You exceed expectations. Those ranked rather highly among my servants," a voice boomed around her.

"...Dark Lord?!"

The will-o'-the-wisps lighting up the corridor went out at once.

"You pass the test. I shall permit you an audience with me."

And as soon as the voice said that, a white glowing magical circle appeared beneath Sakuya.

"What...? Aaah!"

◆

What? Did Sakuya's Holy Sword just change?

Leonis cocked an eyebrow, still seated on his throne of bones. He knew, of course, that Holy Swords were capable of Mode Shifting, a transformation that altered their configuration. For example, Regina's Drag Howl could go from a cannon to a sniper rifle. However, Sakuya had never used that dark lightning during training matches.

Is this some kind of last resort she wouldn't employ while sparring?

Perhaps there was a cost to Mode Shifting. Or maybe Sakuya

had some other reason to keep it secret? Leonis looked down from his throne as a magic circle appeared in the center of the room, teleporting Sakuya into his audience chamber.

"Where am I?" the flustered girl demanded, looking around.

"Conduct yourself accordingly, for you are in the presence of the Dark Lord Zol Vadis," Leonis declared loudly. He'd already donned his Dark Lord's mask and had Shary and Blackas step away.

"You have quite the crude way of handling a lady," Sakuya remarked, watching the disguised Leonis with reproach.

"Given that you are an intruder, I'd say I treated you in a most gentlemanly fashion," Leonis shot back.

Sakuya bit her lip. "I apologize for my intrusion. I simply thought this would be the only way to meet you."

"I see. Then what brings you to my castle?"

Sakuya lowered Raikirimaru slightly and replied, "Dark Lord, you said you're this city's ruler. That you control it from the shadows."

"Indeed. Whether you humans admit it or not, the Seventh Assault Garden is already my—"

"In that case, surely anyone who tries to destroy this city is your enemy, right?" Sakuya cut in.

"Hmm." Leonis narrowed his eyes. "Are you saying someone aims to destroy my kingdom?"

"I don't know what they're plotting for sure, but I do know that it's bound to be terrible. And those people are likely the same ones who smuggled in the Voids you annihilated at the pier yesterday."

"Oh?" Leonis frowned beneath his mask. "You claim they were brought in? I thought the Voids crept out of the emptiness."

"Yes, at least...I think they did." Sakuya shook her head. Evidently, she had no proof about this, either.

"Assuming you're right, and those people did bring Voids into my domain, then their actions are a clear act of hostility toward me."

"Dark Lord Zol Vadis," Sakuya entreated, looking directly at him. "I want to stop them, but I won't be able to do this on my own."

"You seek my strength?"

"...Yes," Sakuya replied, her expression strained with concern.

"Are the people you speak of powerful?"

"They are. Although they're few in number, each is a Holy Swordsman on the same level as me. And they fight without fear of death."

Leonis nodded. "I see."

A group of Holy Swordsmen on par with Sakuya, hm...?

A group like that would make for wonderful servants. However...

"Anyone who menaces my kingdom—be it Voids or Holy Swordsmen—is an enemy of mine," Leonis declared, his voice echoing ominously through the room. "You shall have my aid. Know, however, that if you ask a Dark Lord for help, you must be prepared to pay a suitable price."

"..." Sakuya bit her lip anxiously. "Do you mean some kind of sexual demand...?"

"No!" Leonis called out, flustered.

"Oh, that's good." Sakuya sighed with relief.

"Sakuya Sieglinde. I order that you and the people of the Sakura Orchid join my army."

"...You want me to be your subordinate?"

"Correct. I will induct you into the Dark Lords' Armies as a guest general."

"I don't think someone as mighty as you requires my power."

"Do you? Well, I hold your capabilities in high esteem."

"And you want the people of the Sakura Orchid, too...?"

"Yes." Leonis nodded grandly on his throne. "They shall all enter into the service of the Dark Lords' Armies."

"Are you asking us to turn against the Integrated Human Empire?"

"That's what it would entail, yes."

"..." Sakuya bit her lip again and stared at Leonis for a moment. "If you were only requesting my loyalty, I'd accept. However, the people of the Sakura Orchid cannot serve you," she stated decisively.

"I see..."

Sakuya didn't mind allying herself with him. That in and of itself was a pained decision that took a great deal of resolve for the young woman to make. She was obviously prepared to defend the Seventh Assault Garden to the last, even if it meant selling her soul to a Dark Lord.

Leonis shook his head. "We have nothing more to discuss, then."

"Dark Lord!"

"I want the Sakura Orchid itself. If you're unwilling to accept my offer..."

Leonis raised his hands and snapped his fingers.

"W-wait, what are you—aaaah!"

Countless umbral tendrils coiled around Sakuya's body and began dragging her into the dark.

"Think on my offer. Should you change your mind, come to my castle again."

With a dripping sound, the girl was pulled into the shadows and sent through one of the portals located below the surface of the Seventh Assault Garden.

Now then...

"What do you think of Sakuya's words?" Leonis asked Blackas, who had been hiding in the darkness.

"You mean about the people who smuggled Voids into the city? Hmm. It's suspicious. It's possible they're connected with Zemein and that whelp, Nefakess."

"I agree that this activity exceeds the boundaries of mere terrorists. It's like that suspicious witch, Sharnak, who manipulated the Sovereign Wolves into abducting the princess."

"What are you planning to do then, Lord Magnus? Will you leave them be?"

"Of course not."

Leonis removed his Dark Lord's mask and flashed a diabolical smile. This attack on the Seventh Assault Garden was tantamount to challenging the Undead King himself. Sakuya didn't even need to ask him to do it. He would've crushed them thoroughly either way.

"Foolish humans. You will rue the day you incurred my wrath."

◆

"Nothing seems to go the way I want it to," the young bishop groaned as he moved pieces on a game board. "I do hate games with too many uncertainty factors."

There wasn't anyone on the opposite side of the board, only the boundless emptiness of the void.

He was in a prismatic space located within the Void territory. There stood a gate with a silver lock. It was the deepest of blanknesses, which connected with all of space-time.

The Otherworldly Castle. The seat of one of the eight Dark Lords, Azra-Ael.

There, the Void Bishop, Nefakess Reizaad, complained to himself. The old man who had previously occupied the other side of this board had died in a fight the other day.

"Well, so be it. It is a bit boring without someone to play with, but..." Nefakess lifted his eyes from the board. "Even so, it was an unexpected development. To think that the Undead King had *already been destroyed*."

That was a deviation from the future outlined in the prophecy. Not being able to turn the greatest of Dark Lords into their pawn was a major setback. On top of that, the experiment with the Holy Woman of the Six Heroes had failed, and Veira, the Dragon Lord, had been defeated, too...

"Are all these uncertain factors having some kind of influence on causality...?" Nefakess wondered aloud.

As he thought about it, he realized that his plans had started going awry ever since the Archsage Arakael went berserk.

"The Seventh Assault Garden, that sanctuary of humanity. Something there is causing this."

Riselia Crystalia. He'd planted a fragment of the goddess in that vampire girl to be on the safe side.

Perhaps it's not her, but one she serves...?

Nefakess had to consider every contingency when it came to the future the goddess had foretold.

"It seems we'll need to meddle with destiny a bit."

"Do you intend on making Shardark into a vessel for the goddess, even after he succumbed to nothingness?" a voice called from the darkness.

"Ah, if it isn't Lord Gisark," Nefakess remarked with a grin.

The Divine Dragon of the Six Heroes appeared silently behind him.

"You should not interfere with him," Gisark cautioned. "He has taken in countless gods, as well as Dizolf, the Lord of Rage. He's far too unstable to be a vessel."

"Yes, that might be true."

"He is a hero who fell to the emptiness to destroy the goddess. The Swordmaster of the Six Heroes may have become a singularity that is bending the fate of the prophecy."

"If that's true, could we not reap the benefits of that open seam in causality?" Nefakess wondered, picking up one of the game pieces and toying with it.

"Don't grow conceited, bishop. The only one who can weave the strings of fate is the goddess."

"Yes, I'm aware of that, of course. All is according to the goddess's will."

The bishop turned, but there wasn't anyone there anymore by the time he did.

CHAPTER 5

THE DARK LORD EXPLORES THE SAKURA ORCHID

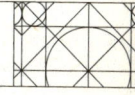

One day, nine years ago, a red star appeared in the sky. It formed quite irregularly, without reason or regard for the turn of the heavens. The empire called it the Star of Calamity. The Sakura Orchid named it the Star of Misfortune.

When it formed, the sky split in two, and Voids spilled from the massive fissure in space. This cataclysmic rush of Voids washed over the Sakura Orchid, destroying its capital and devouring its people.

Amid the chaos, two girls—one six, the other thirteen—raced through the burning streets. The sisters looked very similar, with their striking blue hair.

"Sister…I…I can't run any longer!"

Young Sakuya fell over, rolling over the rubble.

"On your feet." Her older sister turned around and grabbed her arm tight. "If you don't keep moving, the Voids will kill you."

"But is there anywhere to go? Mother and Father, they're… they're already… Nnng…"

Sakuya balled her hands and started weeping.

"The strongest of our land, the Kenki Gathering, are still alive. For now, we must reach Raiou—"

Setsura cut herself short and looked around. Sakuya followed her gaze and spied a lone figure. He was a tall, dashing man with long blond hair. A patch covered his left eye, and he wore a long coat. In his hands was a single-edged broadsword.

It was obvious from his appearance that he wasn't from the Sakura Orchid. Even more peculiar was how he stood in the middle of the hellish scene without the slightest concern.

"So you two are the Priestesses of the Twin Gods."

"...?!"

The stranger lifted his weapon and approached them slowly, an oily miasma rising around his body. He had the same horrifying presence as those monsters...

"Sakuya, run," Setsura instructed, spreading out her arms to shield her sister. "If nothing else, you have to—"

"No, sister...!"

Blood was scattered through the air like petals from a wilting tree. Setsura's body went flying, and then hit the ground hard.

"No... Nooo! Sisterrrrrrrrrrrrrrrrrr!"

A crimson puddle formed on the shattered flagstones. Sakuya hurried over to her sister and took her hand.

"Saku...ya... No... R-run..."

As Sakuya clung to Setsuna, sobbing, a large shadow eclipsed her.

"Priestesses of the Twin Gods, I must eliminate all of the Goddess Factors without exception."

"...?!"

"You..." Sakuya's eyesight, blurred by tears as it was, focused on the monster lording over her. "Who are you? Why? Why did you do this to Setsura?!"

"The emptiness has no name," the one-eyed man said coldly. "But once... Long ago, I was known as Shardark."

"Shardark..." Sakuya mouthed his name like a curse. "That's... That's your name..."

But what did learning it achieve? After all, this nothingness in human form would claim her life in just a moment.

"If nothing else, priestess, I will ensure you die without pain."

And then, that man—that monster—swung his sword down at Sakuya's neck.

◆

"Aaah...! Haah, haah...!"

Sakuya jolted awake in her room in Hræsvelgr dorm. Her sleeping gown clung to her skin from sweat.

It feels like it's been a while since I dreamt of that day...

After wiping her forehead, Sakuya opened the curtains. It was still dark out, but the sunlight was just barely beginning to encroach on the night sky. Sakuya stood in front of her dresser mirror and undressed.

Examining herself, she got the feeling her modest bosom had grown a bit. A face that resembled her late older sister's stared back at her from the glass. If Sakuya were to grow out her hair, she would surely be indistinguishable from Setsura.

What should I do?

Sakuya put on a bra, noting how it felt a bit tighter than it ought to, and heaved a sigh. The Kenki Gathering hadn't contacted her since their first warning. Sakuya had sent Eika to search for their hideout, but she hadn't had any luck thus far.

Naturally, Sakuya had no intention of going along with the Kenki Gathering's plan. Regardless of their intentions, she couldn't let them endanger this city's populace.

After failing to protect the Sakura Orchid, the Kenki Gathering became obsessed with vengeance.

And I'm no different, Sakuya reminded herself bitterly.

After all, her body was a vessel, the same power of emptiness that the monsters she swore to vanquish used.

I wish I could've convinced him...

The Kenki Gathering was a group of powerful Holy Swordsmen. Sakuya stood no chance against them on her own. Regrettably, she had failed to convince the Dark Lord to render aid. Sakuya simply couldn't accept his conditions. She was willing to give herself to him, but turning over the people of the Sakura Orchid left her no option but to refuse.

Maybe I should consider myself lucky he didn't simply kill me right then and there.

If he'd wanted, that Dark Lord likely could've done it easily.

He was more gentlemanly than I expected, though. Or maybe he has something else in mind...

As she thought on it, Sakuya donned the white garb of her homeland—a memento of her sister.

"Setsura, please... Watch over the Sakura Orchid."

◆

"Mm... Ah..."

It was early morning. Having gotten plenty of sleep, Leonis awakened and rubbed his bleary eyes. When he opened the curtain and peered outside, he saw Sakuya practicing with her sword.

It's about time I get going...

Leonis slipped out of bed and crept quietly from the room to keep from waking Riselia.

Yesterday certainly was a spectacular failure.

As he descended the staircase, Leonis let out a disappointed exhale. It wasn't the matter with Sakuya that vexed him, but the body double he'd left at Tessera's birthday party.

After concluding his matters in the castle, Leonis had returned to the orphanage at once to relieve Dorug. But during his one-hour absence, the Champion of Rognas had managed to mess things up quite spectacularly.

When Dorug was informed that people sing and give presents at birthday celebrations, he launched into the Dark Fanfare. The tune's lyrics praised the Dark Lords' Armies. Even worse, he performed the entire song with great enthusiasm and wholly off key.

Just remembering the awkward atmosphere Leonis had walked into when he got back made him wish he could bury himself.

"E-everyone has things they're bad at, Leo!" Riselia had said, clearly hoping to console him.

"That's right!" Regina agreed. "Let's go to a karaoke place and practice together, okay kid?"

"I—I was happy you sang for me, Leo...," Tessera admitted bashfully.

But their every attempt at encouragement was another twist of the knife.

Incidentally, Arle had apparently disappeared after eating some food. Perhaps she'd feared Riselia and the others might catch and interrogate her if she remained too long.

I suppose that's the only silver lining here.

Had she remained and heard Dorug sing the Dark Fanfare, it would have exposed Leonis's identity.

Damn you, Dorug! I should take away that Ironblood Death Medal I gave you for your service in the Siege of Zaras!

Leonis made his way to the concourse outside the dormitory. He could hear the sound of something cutting through the air.

And standing under an artificial broadleaf tree, made for purifying sweet water, was...

"Haaaaaaa!"

Sakuya held Raikirimaru at the ready. Her blade flashed several times, slicing through multiple leaves that had dropped from branches before they touched the ground.

This is quite hackneyed, as training goes.

Upon close inspection, however, the fallen leaves were elaborately cut into the shapes of animals and geometric petals.

...Her swordsmanship skills are far beyond Riselia's.

"Who's there?" Sakuya asked, turning around.

"Good morning, Miss Sakuya." Leonis approached her and bowed politely.

"What is it, kid? You're not usually up so early."

"...Yes. Actually, I wanted to ask you for a favor."

"A favor? And it's one you want to keep secret from Miss Selia..." Sakuya paused and thought for a moment. "Is it something pervy?"

"No," Leonis replied at once.

Is this girl sexually frustrated or something?

"It isn't? I suppose I jumped to conclusions."

"Very much so. Um, I'm supposed to take Tessera, a friend of mine from the orphanage, to the Sakura Orchid Festival. I was hoping you could introduce me to places in Old Town, so I could show her around."

This was Leonis's convenient excuse. His true objective was to gather information on the deities worshipped by the Sakura Orchid's people. With any luck, it would provide clues to the goddess he sought.

There was also the matter of the group Sakuya had mentioned

yesterday. Leonis couldn't ignore that, and he thought that it might be better to inquire about it as himself and not the Dark Lord Zol Vadis.

"Oh, so you're going to watch the enshrinement ritual?"

"Yes, I've heard you'll be performing there as a shrine maiden."

"Well, yes. Though knowing you'll be watching is a bit embarrassing..." Sakuya scratched her cheek. "But all right, I'll show you around. I was planning to go back to the estate and practice the dance anyway."

◆

And so Leonis decided that he and Sakuya would meet after his morning lectures, so that Riselia wouldn't scold him.

Sakuya didn't have a vehicle license, and so the pair had to take the shuttle bus to Old Town. They got off in the Area II Station, and walked the rest of the way there.

"Isn't Miss Selia worried about you, though?"

"It's fine. My terminal has the guardian function installed on it, so she can track where I am."

"...I see. Miss Selia is a bit overprotective, isn't she?"

"Very," Leonis replied.

"My lord, my lord—" a voice abruptly called in his mind.

Shary was watching Leonis from somewhere. Looking around, he spotted a girl in a maid's outfit standing atop a nearby building. It was a conspicuous spot, but Shary had concealed her presence, so most people wouldn't notice her.

"Is something wrong, Shary?"

"No, it's just that if you wanted to investigate the area, I could've done it for you."

...It seemed she didn't feel comfortable with Leonis coming here himself. Even at this distance, he spotted her puffing up her cheeks in an adorable pout.

"*I don't doubt your abilities. I simply think there are some things you can only understand by seeing the place yourself,*" Leonis explained.

"*...I see. As prudent as ever, my lord,*" Shary replied sagely and bowed from her perch on the rooftop. "*So you wish to find the best sweet shops based on your personal taste.*"

"No, that's not it," Leonis unintentionally responded aloud.

"What isn't it, kid?" Sakuya, who was walking beside Leonis, cast a confused look at him.

"Oh, nothing," Leonis said evasively.

Before long, they arrived at the gate leading into Old Town. The atmosphere beyond felt like that of an entirely different world. There were still some skyscrapers, but there were far more wooden buildings along the road.

"Once you cross through, you'll be in the Sakura Orchid's self-governed area," Sakuya pointed out.

She and Leonis held up their ID cards and entered.

"Were these buildings relocated from the Sakura Orchid?" Leonis inquired.

"No, they were built here," Sakuya replied sadly. "The capital was completely razed in the Stampede nine years ago. Only the shrine and the worship stone were salvaged."

Leonis lowered his head. "...I'm sorry. That was an insensitive question."

"Oh, don't worry. For a young boy, you're very considerate." Sakuya giggled, seemingly amused. "Now, let's go. And be careful, there are vehicles running..."

She took Leonis's hand and pulled him along.

"M-Miss Sakuya, you don't have to hold my hand."

"Heh-heh. What, are you that embarrassed to hold hands with a girl?"

"...Yes," Leonis responded, his cheeks a bit red.

"Well, you'll get used to it. Now, let's go."

"Huh, wait—Miss Sakuya!"

◆

"The main road leads right to the shrine," Sakuya said while she guided Leonis down the street.

At first, he was embarrassed to have her hold his hand in public, but as she'd stated, he grew accustomed to it quickly. A boy being led by someone older on a busy street wasn't that unusual.

...I guess I'm just being overly self-conscious.

Sakuya looked like she was moving at a relaxed pace, but in truth, she had adjusted her steps to match Leonis's. It suggested a more mature side to the young woman that Leonis hadn't recognized in her previously.

"There's a lot of people," he noted, looking around.

There weren't quite as many passersby as there had been the other day, when he'd shown Veira, the Dragon Lord, around the Central Garden's amusement area. Still, the pedestrian traffic was quite active. He spotted no small number of people in Excalibur Academy uniforms.

"Yes, the atmosphere is a lot calmer than in Central Garden. There are many general stores and confectionaries here, too, so it's a popular spot."

"...I see."

No wonder Shary gave me so many reports about this area in particular.

As they walked on, Leonis noticed something else that surprised him.

"Most people here aren't dressed the same way you are."

Shopkeepers were dressed in Sakura Orchid traditional attire, but most of those walking around weren't.

"The majority of the people here work in the city center," Sakuya explained.

Ah, that stands to reason.

After continuing along the main street for a bit, Leonis and Sakuya arrived at a circular plaza with a fountain. Standing in front of the water feature was a statue fashioned after a wolf.

Is this some manner of gargoyle? Leonis wondered. He sensed no mana coming from it, however, so it had to be an ordinary sculpture.

Noticing Leonis's gaze, Sakuya said, "Wolves are worshipped in the Sakura Orchid as guardian beasts. The shrine has at least twenty-four of them."

She then patted the statue affectionately on the head.

"Doesn't it remind you of Fluffymaru the Black?" she asked.

"Hmm..." It honestly didn't, but Leonis only offered a vague muttering in response. "Speaking of, why did you call that dog Fluffymaru the Black?"

"I call most fluffy things Fluffymaru," Sakuya answered, holding up an index finger for some reason.

"So if you find a sponge..."

"I call it Fluffymaru, yes."

"And if you have a feather pillow..."

"That's Fluffymaru, too!"

"..."

Leonis concluded it would be for the best to simply not think about it.

"By the way, boy, are you hungry yet?"

"Yes, a little."

He'd had breakfast, but they'd walked for a while, so he was beginning to feel peckish.

This body is so inefficient.

"It's still too early for lunch, so let's have a snack in that shop, shall we?" proposed Sakuya.

"Yes. But keep it a secret from Miss Selia, would you?"

She would scold him if she heard he had a snack before lunch.

"Very well. It'll be our secret." Sakuya closed one eye in a wink and brought a finger to her lips.

And so Leonis and Sakuya entered a confectionary store near the plaza and bought a treat called taiyaki. This was one sweet Shary had taken quite a liking to, and she often brought a few to Leonis as souvenirs from her investigations.

"So this fish-shaped snack is originally from the Sakura Orchid," Leonis remarked as they sat on a bench in the plaza.

Sakuya tore her taiyaki in two and then offered its head to Leonis.

"…?" Leonis looked at her, taken aback.

"I'll offer you half of my chocolate taiyaki for half of your custard one. Deal?"

"Oh, yes, deal," Leonis agreed, splitting his own taiyaki in half and handing its head over to Sakuya.

"Heh-heh, I always wanted to try both of them together. I can't exactly do this alone, after all," Sakuya said, pressing the head and the body of the two different taiyaki together in an attempt to make a whole.

"…That's kind of childish, Sakuya," Leonis commented, cracking a wry smile as he took a bite out of his own taiyaki.

The flavorful cream melted in his mouth.

"...That's rich, coming from a child," Sakuya replied as she scooped up a bit of cream that clung to Leonis's cheek with a finger and licked it off.

"...!" Leonis's cheeks flushed.

"What's wrong, boy?" Sakuya inquired with obvious curiosity. Her cluelessness set this apart from Regina's usual brand of teasing.

"By the way, Miss Sakuya..." To change the subject, Leonis brought up something he was curious about. "You were a...princess in the Sakura Orchid, right?"

The blue-haired girl shrugged. "...Mm. Well, not anymore."

"I'm just surprised that the people around here treat you normally."

None of the those passing by called out to Sakuya in particular, and the shopkeeper didn't seem to give her any special treatment despite her royal background. A thousand years ago, that would have been unthinkable. The rigid class system would have forbidden it.

"Well, some of the family's old retainers still call me princess, but we're in the Seventh Assault Garden, and I'm a student at Excalibur Academy, so my origin doesn't matter much," Sakuya explained coolly. "We're all knights, fighting to protect humanity from our common enemy, the Voids."

...I see. I suppose that makes sense.

As Leonis thought on this, he realized that Regina concealed her royal lineage, and Riselia was the daughter of a duke, making her a noble. Similarly, Elfiné's father owned a major conglomerate in the capital. And despite all that, they were all treated as ordinary students in the academy.

Putting aside fools like Viscount Muselle, Excalibur Academy's students didn't seem to place much importance on class or pedigree. Regina only called Riselia "lady" because of her history as the other girl's maid.

"That's why I present myself not with the royal family's name, but with our Imperial name, Sieglinde. It's the proof of my resolve to be reborn as a warrior for Excalibur Academy," Sakuya stated as she stared up at the clear blue sky.

CHAPTER 6

THE TWIN GODS

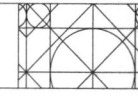

Leonis and Sakuya crossed a coupling bridge built over a river and reached a quieter part of Old Town. At the end of the road was a thick forest of artificial trees.

"The shrine where the enshrinement ritual will be held is past these woods," Sakuya told Leonis.

"Hm..."

"What is it?"

"Do the Sakura Orchid's guardian deities *really exist*?" Leonis inquired, trying his best to play the part of an innocent child.

Was it just a legend, or did the ceremony really involve divine beings? That distinction was crucial for Leonis. He had to find out.

Sakuya fell silent for a moment, long enough to make Leonis wonder if his question had offended her.

"The Sakura Orchid's guardian deities exist, yes," she answered, gazing into the woods. "Fuujinki and Raijinki. They have guarded over the Sakura Orchid for its entire three-hundred-year history."

"Two? The Sakura Orchid has a pair of gods?"

"...Yes. Though there's only one of them now."

"Huh...?" Leonis asked dubiously.

Sakuya stopped in her tracks in front of a large estate with an impressive gate.

"Where are we?" Leonis questioned.

"This estate is where Raiou, my legal guardian, lives."

A magical apparatus authenticated their biometric data, after which the gate opened. Ahead was a large garden dotted with well-tended trees and a sizable pond. It was the kind of place one would've never found in the Central Garden, with its many laminated buildings. Leonis couldn't disguise his admiration as he beheld the sight.

A small old man appeared from within the manor. "—We've been expecting you, Princess Sakuya."

Oh...

Leonis regarded the man with great interest. At first glance, he might have appeared as an ordinary elderly person, but Leonis could tell he was more.

This is a master of martial arts.

His old, dried arms could easily kill someone. He wasn't so much a warrior as he was an assassin.

...Perhaps I can make him into a skilled skeleton assassin after he passes away, Leonis mused, not overly concerned with how rude that notion was.

"My apologies, I was a little late. I was showing him around Old Town," Sakuya replied.

The old man turned his eyes to Leonis.

"Princess Sakuya, who is this boy...?"

"He's Leonis, a member of my platoon."

"Ah, yes, I've heard of him."

Bowing his head politely, Leonis stated, "Miss Sakuya is always a very dependable friend."

"Do come in," the old man said, ushering them inside. "I'll have some tea prepared for you at once."

◆

After being shown into the manor, Leonis took a seat on a veranda that offered a view of the pond. There was a garden on Excalibur Academy's grounds as well, but this one was completely different. It was meant to reproduce the scenery of the Sakura Orchid's lost homeland.

"The roadside trees in the Seventh Assault Garden are utility plants meant to purify sea water and regulate the environment, but those in this garden were all brought from the Sakura Orchid," Sakuya commented as she approached Leonis from behind and pointed at one of the trees growing in the garden. "They sprout beautiful flowers come spring, but the Seventh Assault Garden is an offensive-type colony that travels all over the world, which throws off the timing for the blossoms."

"...I see."

"My older sister always looked forward to seeing those flowers bloom," Sakuya said, her tone and eyes seeming distant.

"..."

Sakuya's sister had perished on the day the Sakura Orchid was destroyed. The white garb she wore under her uniform was a memento of her lost sibling.

A gust of wind blew, and the leaves on the garden's trees rustled. A large ripple played over the surface of the pond—

Splaaaaaaaaash!

Suddenly, a black mass breached the surface.

"...What?!" Leonis exclaimed in surprise.

Sakuya, however, didn't look taken aback.

"Oh, you're here, too, Fluffymaru," she observed with a smile.

A large black wolf stepped out of the pond, his fur drenched, and then shook himself dry, splashing water all over the ground. The beast met Leonis's gaze.

"Oh, it's you, Lord Magnus."

"Blackas, what are you doing here?" Leonis replied to his friend's telepathic greeting.

"Bathing. The humans tend to be surprised when I swim in the academy's pool."

"Yes, I imagine they would be."

"Someone recently reported my presence there, and they very nearly sent another to hunt me down."

"I...see. It seems you've been through a lot."

Blackas was apparently being pursued by Excalibur Academy's hunters' association. Unlike Leonis, who was enrolled in the school, and Shary, who had a human form, Blackas always stood out when he went about his business on his own. There were spells that could give one a humanoid shape. However, Blackas had *unique circumstances* that made that impossible.

"Fluffymaru frequently comes by the estate to play. I would have liked to keep him here, but Raiou said that taming an animal like him would be impossible..."

"...Yes, I feel the same way."

Blackas was the proud prince of the Realm of Shadows, putting him above obeying others. His relationship with Leonis was one of camaraderie. He was a guest general in Leonis's army and by no means a subordinate to the Undead King.

And that proud prince lay sprawled out comfortably under a cherry blossom tree.

"—Here is your tea." Raiou, the old man from earlier, was carrying a tray with a few cups and sweets.

"Thank you."

"I'll go practice for the dance, then," Sakuya stated, getting to her feet. That was why she'd come here to begin with, after all. "I'll return to the estate during the evening, but if you want to go home alone, you should take the bus. You've ridden alone before, right?"

"Yes, I'll be fine. Thank you very much."

"Don't worry, I had fun on my date with you, kid. There's still plenty of places I haven't shown you, so next time we visit, let's take it slow."

◆

"So what do you think of the Sakura Orchid's scenery?"

Raiou sat across from Leonis, sipping his tea.

"It's fascinating. I'm looking forward to the festival."

"That's good to hear," the elderly man replied. He turned his attention to the black wolf lying in the garden. "Princess Sakuya has changed a bit, as of late."

"...Has she?"

"Yes. When she first arrived, her heart was like ice. She'd shut herself off from everyone else."

Leonis didn't know what Sakuya was like back then. But if anything could have thawed her frozen heart, it must surely have been...

...*Riselia, no doubt*, he concluded.

"That reminds me, I wanted to ask you something," Leonis said. After drinking from his cup, he placed it on the floor of the veranda.

If Raiou was a vassal of the Sakura Orchid's royal family, he surely knew all sorts of things on the matter.

"Yes?"

"What kind of gods are the Sakura Orchid's guardian deities?"

"Hmm. Are you interested in our religion?"

"Miss Sakuya told me a bit about it. She said the Sakura Orchid was protected by two gods."

"...Yes, that's correct."

Raiou turned around and pointed at a pillar supporting the estate.

"They are carved into that column over there. Fuujinki and Raijinki."

"Over there...?"

Looking up the pillar, Leonis saw carvings of two giants glaring down from atop the clouds.

"Their names stand for that which they govern over. Raijinki commands thunder and Fuujinki calls great storms. Whenever the Sakura Orchid faced crises, they would wield their powers to protect the land."

"Then you mean to say those deities existed?"

"Of course. The gods of the Sakura Orchid aren't simply fictional beings of legend," Raiou stated, and he shook his head. "I saw it with my own two eyes. How the Twin Gods did battle with the Voids."

Nine years ago, when the Void Stampede washed over the Sakura Orchid, the royal family broke the seals on the two gods in an attempt to beat the Voids back. They believed that with their mighty powers, Raijinki and Fuujinki would annihilate the monsters and save the Sakura Orchid—

"However, just when it seemed that faint hope was within reach, *it* appeared."

Raiou was referring to the Void Lord who had caused the Stampede. It emerged from the emptiness and defeated the two gods in a matter of minutes. And then, it consumed and absorbed the defeated Fuujinki.

"It devoured...a god?" Leonis was struck with disbelief.

"Indeed. That monster took Fuujinki into its being."

And with the storm god fused into it, the Void Lord could freely abuse its divine authority. Thus was the Sakura Orchid overrun by the Voids, ending its three-hundred-year-long history.

...I think I understand now.

Based on this story, Leonis was able to form a hypothesis on what the Sakura Orchid's divine protectors were.

They were probably demi-gods.

Demi-gods were subordinate entities produced by the Luminous Powers. While they were no match for true gods, they did possess terrifying powers. Leonis could remember how, in the past, demi-gods gave the Dark Lords' Armies a great deal of trouble.

...There was still something Leonis didn't understand yet, though. If one of the gods, Fuujinki, was devoured by the Void Lord...

"What happened to the other deity?" Leonis asked.

"While the Void Lord consumed Fuujinki, Princess Setsura sealed Raijinki, who was grievously injured in the fight. I'm certain she believed the Sakura Orchid would have truly met its demise if its final guardian was lost."

"...I'm inclined to agree."

Among the countries the Dark Lords' Armies had destroyed, Leonis faced a ruler who, as foolish as it was, and as clear as defeat may have been, opposed him to the last. They believed that so long as they didn't accept defeat, they could always find a way to turn the tables.

Just like Roselia, whose soul endured, even after one thousand years.

"Without its greatest protectors on the battlefield, the Sakura Orchid fell to ruin. That swarm of demons crushed our fortresses and invaded the capital, intending to swallow our land entirely. The capital was guarded by a group of Holy Swordsmen known as the Kenki Gathering, but they were overwhelmed by sheer numbers. Ultimately, they failed to safeguard Princess Setsura—Princess Sakuya's older sister."

Raiou's features contorted with grief and regret. Leonis knew his feelings all too well—pain at having failed to protect what mattered most. Unfortunately, he couldn't sympathize out loud.

"That is how the Twin Gods of the Sakura Orchid became just one—Raijinki," Raiou concluded.

A gust of wind rustled the trees.

"So the surviving deity remains in the former lands of the Sakura Orchid?" Leonis questioned.

Raiou shook his head and pointed down. "No."

"Huh?" Leonis knit his brows, unclear on what to make of the gesture.

"Our guardian god is sealed right here, in the Seventh Assault Garden," the old man declared.

◆

After leaving the estate, Sakuya made her way to the relocated grove leading up to the shrine. Her steps were lighter than usual. She'd been terribly tense recently, but the date with Leonis was just the change of pace she'd needed.

It wasn't long, but I did have fun.

The familiar sights of Old Town felt a bit different when she walked by his side.

Perhaps I should take him to more confectionary stores next time. But I'll probably need Miss Selia's permission, and she can be overprotective...

Smiling at that thought, she set foot in the overgrown grounds of the shrine, when suddenly—

"Princess Sakuya."

"...?!"

Sakuya suddenly became aware of several presences in the woods. The girl stopped in her tracks and scanned the trees. She couldn't see them, but they were definitely there. This could be the work of only one group.

The Kenki Gathering...

Sakuya counted five, six of them...perhaps even more.

"You're intruding upon the priestess princess's holy ground. Are you trying to get yourselves cursed by the heavens?"

"We're aware of how blasphemous this is. But no one will interrupt us here."

The darkness took form and surfaced before her eyes, becoming a figure in a black anti-Void protection suit. Unlike the man who spoke to her yesterday, this one wasn't using a voice changer, and his tone was familiar.

"Is that you, Uzan?" Sakuya asked. "I remember you playing with me when I was still a little girl."

"It's been a long time, Princess Sakuya." The man kneeled respectfully, displaying a retainer's fealty.

Despite the gesture, Sakuya didn't relax.

"You could at least try to mask your Demon Sword's presence," she stated firmly. "I sense the power of a Demon Sword in all of you."

One of those behind Uzan stirred at her remark.

"...I see you are familiar with Demon Swords," Uzan said.

"Where did you get that power? You do know that using it contaminates your body with nothingness, right?"

Uzan's answer was immediate. "Of course we do, Princess Sakuya."

"Then why...?!"

"Because we need the strength it offers if we are to achieve our revenge and make our heart's desire a reality."

"Revenge..." Sakuya's eyes widened in shock. "Just what are you plotting?"

"Nothing less than our ultimate objective."

"What?"

"We will summon the Void Lord who destroyed the Sakura Orchid nine years ago to this land."

"...Wh-what?!"

◆

"The Sakura Orchid's god is sealed here in the Seventh Assault Garden?" Leonis was utterly astonished.

"I can't blame you for being surprised, but it is the truth."

"..."

During his reign as the Undead King, Leonis fought many gods. But while the mega-float the Seventh Assault Garden sat upon was quite vast, he didn't detect any traces of a sealed divine entity.

If there was a god here, Blackas and I would have surely noticed it by now. Though I suppose it's possible we may have overlooked one in a dormant state...

Then he realized something.

...It can't be!

Leonis recalled that he had encountered a mass of super-high-density mana the likes of which had never existed in his era. It was a source capable of producing enough magical power to support all the functions of this mobile city and its population of over one million people.

"...The Mana Furnace!"

Raiou nodded. "Precisely. The Integrated Human Empire unearthed Raijinki from the ruins of the Sakura Orchid and placed our guardian in the Mana Furnace that serves as the heart of this city."

...I see. So this city uses a god as the power source.

Such a feat was unthinkable one thousand years ago. The idea of mere humans harnessing superior beings and using them for energy... It did clear up a few previously unanswered questions, though.

Why was there such a large mana crystal? Why did the Archsage Arakael and the Holy Woman Tearis Resurrectia try to merge with Mana Furnaces?

The Six Heroes weren't inherently drawn to the Mana Furnaces; they were trying to absorb the gods within them.

...I may have underestimated what humanity is capable of.

Surely this wasn't limited to just the Seventh Assault Garden. The others were likely powered by ancient gods, too.

And since they're using the deities, those in charge must have wiped all records of their existence...

Leonis fixed his gaze on Raiou. "Did Sakuya and the people of the Sakura Orchid...agree to this?"

"The circumstances are different, but one of our Twin Gods is still protecting the Sakura Orchid's populace. That much hasn't changed...," Raiou replied. "And very few people know the truth. Only the military's top brass and those close to the Sakura Orchid's royal family. And now you as well..."

"...!"

Indeed, this was information Leonis had never come across, despite his previous research.

"...Why share this secret with me?"

"I pride myself on having a good eye for people." Raiou smiled and peered into Leonis's eyes.

...My word. A good eye for people, he says? Perhaps he should have his vision examined. I'm a Dark Lord, an enemy of humankind...

Blackas, who was lying in the garden, suddenly raised his head, his ears pricking up.

"What's wrong, Blackas?" Leonis asked telepathically.

"Several strange presences have appeared around the girl."

"...What?"

◆

"...You're going to summon the Void Lord here?" Sakuya was incredulous. "Don't tell me you're trying to cause a Stampede here?!"

"That's right, Princess Sakuya," Uzan replied without remorse. "We thirty-seven Kenki Gathering members will call our sworn enemy, Shardark Void Lord, and strike him down."

"..."

The unwavering faith, the confidence in his voice, filled Sakuya with terror.

"B-but how would you even...?"

"By unleashing the seal on Raijinki, the Twin God slumbering in this city's Mana Furnace," Uzan declared, emotion peeking through in his voice for the first time.

"What...?"

"Surely you know this already, Princess Sakuya. That Void Lord absorbed Fuujinki. However, the Sakura Orchid's deities are two parts of a whole. If he senses the other half is unleashed, he will surely come for it..."

"..."

Sakuya was aghast.

They're planning to use Raijinki as bait for the Void Lord, so they can slay him?

What was this man saying? It was madness. This couldn't even be called a plan; they were simply looking for somewhere to die. They'd spent too long on the path of carnage, and after hunting Voids for so long, they'd lost sight of all else.

No, perhaps they'd been mad since that day nine years ago...

Once she'd got over her initial astonishment, Sakuya asked, "And you really think you can manage to kill the Void Lord?"

"We've besmirched ourselves with the power of the Voids to that end," Uzan replied, clenching his armored fist. "Shardark Void Lord will fight the unleashed Raijinki, and once he is weakened, we will strike him down. While we don't intend to rely on them, the Stampede caused by the Void Lord's appearance will surely draw the city's Holy Swordsman into the fight as well."

"You're willing to forfeit the Seventh Assault Garden to get your revenge?!" Sakuya cried, furious.

"It will be a sacrifice to stomp out the Voids."

"...Uzan!" Sakuya shouted and manifested Raikirimaru in her hands.

Just like the Kenki Gathering, Sakuya had dedicated her life to revenge. However...

—I will not become a mindless demon... I won't relinquish my human heart!

She gripped her Holy Sword as tendrils of pale lightning raged across its blade.

"The only one who can unleash Raijinki is the princess priestess of the Mikagami royal family—me. Do you think I'd ever agree to your plan?"

"Your refusal is a shame, but our plan will not change. We already have a princess priestess on our side."

"...What?" Sakuya gave Uzan a confused look, but the man didn't bother to clarify.

"Since you've drawn your Holy Sword, I take it to mean there's no room for negotiations anymore."

"That's right. I'll never join you!" Sakuya stepped forward and swung her weapon.

However, her attack was blocked by a *third arm* that sprouted out of Uzan's back.

"...What?!" Sakuya's exclaimed. "Have you truly been corrupted by the nothingness that much...?!"

"You have grown strong, Princess Sakuya. However—" A pair of red eyes glinted behind his helmet. "You're still no match for Princess Setsura."

"...Setsura...?"

A fourth arm sprouted from his back and grabbed Sakuya by the throat.

"Kah...aah..."

The fingers of the monstrous arm dug into her throat. Perhaps Uzan had mentioned her deceased sister's name simply to shake her resolve. It wounded Sakuya to know that the man who was once the Sakura Orchid's most celebrated swordsman had fallen so far...

"...Damn, you...!"

...She couldn't breathe. Her consciousness was growing hazy. Raikirimaru slipped from her fingers and faded into thin air...

"...—kuya... Miss Sakuya!"

But just then, she heard a familiar voice from afar.

"...K-kid... Stay...away...!" the young woman desperately gasped out.

"It seems we've been spotted," one of the Kenki Gathering

members observed. "Lord Uzan, the time has not yet come. Suppress your Demon Sword's power."

"—Yes, understood."

The arm holding her slackened its grip, and Sakuya collapsed to the ground. "...Ugh...," she managed, coughing.

"I wanted you to be a part of our plan, Princess Sakuya," Uzan said, looking down at her. Then he turned away and vanished into the darkness.

"W-wait..."

As her consciousness faded, Sakuya could hear Leonis's voice getting closer.

CHAPTER 7

THE ENSHRINEMENT RITUAL

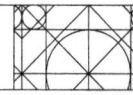

The boy first met the man in a back alley in the slums.

"An orphan. I see..."

"...?"

That boy, covered in rags and kneeling in the muck, gazed up at the tall figure. He was handsome with beautiful blond hair. The man inspected the boy's face. His armor was silver and his cloak, a pure white. A sword adorned with gold decorations hung at his hip.

"...Are you a knight?"

The boy quickly corrected his posture and fell prostrate. Knights were among the highest classes in the Rognas Kingdom, and if a young vagrant like him were to appear disrespectful to the knight, he was within his rights to cut him down where he stood.

But why would such a neat and proper swordsman call out to him...? The boy simply couldn't understand.

"Your soul has a rare, exceptional color to it. The same color as mine—the soul of a hero."

"Huh?"

The knight said something terribly strange.

"Oh, I can see the color of one's soul. It's one of my unique skills."

"The color of one's...soul...?" the boy repeated, dumbfounded.

"What of your family?" the man asked, placing a hand on the boy's shoulder.

"I don't have a family. My brother and sister died in the war."

"—I see. Hearing that saddens me greatly. Our kingdom's knights have failed you."

"N-no, milord! Not at all...!" the boy insisted, alarmed.

He had the feeling this knight's blue eyes could see right through him, down into his very core—and, indeed, his soul.

"How old are you?"

"I'm five... No, probably six."

"Have you ever wielded a sword before?"

The boy shook his head. He'd never so much as held a real sword.

"Good, it's better that way." The man nodded, evidently satisfied. "You haven't developed any needless habits, then."

"Hm...?"

The boy's face clouded over with confusion, but the man reached out to him and finally asked the question.

"Tell me, my boy—would you like to become a hero?"

◆

Beep beep beep beep beep...!

"...Ngh, who dares disturb this Dark Lord's slumber?!"

Still half asleep, Leonis picked up his terminal, which was ringing, and threw it against the wall.

The device bounced and fell to the floor.

"…"

Leonis massaged his temples and sighed. It was almost dusk outside. Two days had passed since Sakuya had shown him around Old Town, making it the day of the enshrinement ritual. Excalibur Academy students were excused from classes today, so after he'd trained with Riselia this morning, Leonis had taken an afternoon nap.

He sat up in his bed, combing his fingers through his unruly hair.

What an unpleasant dream.

…It had been one of that man, of all things. Leonis's teacher and the Swordmaster of the Six Heroes. Most of his memories of his days as a hero had faded… Why did he still have to see him in dreams?

Grimacing, Leonis got out of bed. It was almost time. He needed to get changed, pick Tessera up from the orphanage, and then make his way to Old Town.

…I just hope nothing out of the ordinary happens.

Leonis thought back to what Sakuya had told him.

Members of the Kenki Gathering, an elite group from the Sakura Orchid, had visited Sakuya. They had once been charged with protecting royalty, but like the rest of their people, they'd lost their homeland in the Void Stampede nine years ago.

And now, to exact revenge on the Void Lord responsible, they planned to cause another Stampede here in the Seventh Assault Garden. Sakuya had approached the Dark Lord Zol Vadis for help with stopping them.

This is my kingdom. I wasn't going to let them have their way to begin with.

He currently had Shary and Blackas stationed in Old Town in case anything happened. Additionally, he'd dispatched the Demon

Wolf Pack to track the enemy's movements. They hadn't found any traces of them yet, though.

I'll definitely need to strengthen my intelligence organization in the future.

Blackas was an offensive general who exhibited his full strength on the battlefield, and while Shary was talented in espionage, her true role was assassination and not gathering information. Some of the beastmen species were well suited for spying, but none of the ones working under Leonis had the dedicated skills required.

...At some point, I should recruit people skilled in this sort of thing.

A certain black-haired girl with a Holy Sword optimized for data gathering flashed in his mind, but then...

"Leo, are you awake? It's time to go pick up Tessera."

"Get ready and dress yourself, kid!"

Riselia and Regina called to him from the other side of the door.

◆

"What do you think? Does this yukata look good on me?"

Regina entered and spun in place, showing off her outfit. It wasn't her usual uniform, but a traditional Sakura Orchid outfit called a yukata. Hers was made of pale blue-green fabric and decorated with flower and butterfly patterns. Her hair wasn't done in her usual pigtails. Instead it was tied in a single ponytail.

"H-hm..."

As Regina struck a pose, Leonis hastily averted his gaze. The yukata was very open around the chest and had a sizable slit on its hem. Honestly, it made for a tantalizing sight when a buxom girl like Regina wore it.

"Oh, what are you going red for, kid? Heh heh... ♪" Regina smiled after noticing Leonis's flustered reaction.

She leaned forward and poked Leonis's cheek with a finger.

"...!" He jumped.

Enduring this kind of teasing wounded his dignity as a Dark Lord. And so he turned around and gazed directly at Regina.

"...Hm? K-kid?"

Regina looked a bit confused now that he was staring at her.

"Yes, it suits you very well," he muttered. "That hairdo is very cute on you, too."

"Ah, really? I-it's...cute?" Regina asked, going red.

"Of course, the way you usually look is very cute, too."

"...Ahhhhh, y-you shouldn't tease girls like that, kid."

"I'm not. It's how I really feel..."

"Y-you dummy! You big dumb dummy!" Regina shook her head, face scarlet. Her ponytail wagged side to side.

Regina was the kind of girl who couldn't handle receiving compliments very well.

Leonis had meant every word he said, though. Regina truly did look cute. Reiterating as much would just make her more bashful, however, so Leonis decided not to.

...I dread to think what she might do if I push her too far.

This was Regina, after all, the one who held authority over their dinner menu.

"Lady Selia, it's terrible! The kid is turning into a Dark Lord of the bedroom again!" In the face of an opponent she could not best, Regina went crying to her mistress.

"Yes, yes, now stop fooling around and get ready, you two," Riselia replied a bit absently.

"Get ready how?" Regina asked.

"Both Leo and I still need to change into our yukatas. Here's yours, Leo," Riselia said, taking a neatly folded garment out of her bag. "I rented it from an apparel shop. It should be your size, Leo."

"I'm fine going in my uniform," Leonis protested.

"Out of the question. I want to see you in a—ahem, I mean that's just how this festival works."

"...Oh."

Well, if there were rules, he wasn't going to argue against them. Leonis accepted the yukata reluctantly.

"Am I supposed to just tie the waist sash however I want?" he questioned, spreading the yukata out and looking at it curiously.

"Don't worry, kid, I'll help you," Regina replied, placing her hands on Leonis's shoulders.

"Y-you don't have to. I can put it on by myself."

"No, no, no. We don't have that much time."

"I'll go get changed, then," Riselia stated. "Regina, I'm counting on you to help Leo get dressed."

"Understood, Lady Selia."

Seeing Regina nod encouragingly, Riselia went to her bedroom. No sooner had the door clicked shut than Regina reached for Leonis's shirt.

"Come on, kid, take off your uniform. Or do you want me to remove it for you?"

Realizing that resistance was futile in this situation, Leonis obediently did as he was told.

"Your pants, too," Regina added.

"...I—I know! Just turn around already, Miss Regina!"

Once he was certain Regina wasn't watching, Leonis swiftly took off his trousers and slipped into his yukata.

"Heh-heh, it looks good on you... Oh, you've got the collar on backward. It's supposed to be like this. ♪"

The blond young woman fixed his collar and briskly tied the sash around his waist. Leonis offered no objection until she tightened the sash.

"M-Miss Regina... It's too taut, I can't breathe."

He hadn't felt this suffocated since the Mountain Devouring Dragon attacked Necrozoa and constricted him one thousand years ago.

"Do you want me to loosen it up a little?" Regina inquired, adjusting the sash. "But if it's too loose, it might come undone."

"Leo, are you ready?" The door opened, and Riselia walked in, now clad in her yukata.

"...?!"

Leonis swallowed despite himself. The sight of her in a yukata was quite breathtaking. Hers had black-and-white stripes with flower patterns, and she had her brilliant silver hair done up. This exposed the alluring lines of her neck, giving her usual chaste atmosphere a slightly more enticing feel.

"You look so pretty, Lady Selia!" Regina praised.

"Th-thanks, Regina," Riselia answered, raising one large sleeve to cover her bashful expression.

"...You really do look pretty." The words left Leonis's lips naturally.

"...Boo. You sound more honest than when you complimented me," Regina grumbled.

"Thank you, Leo. Yours looks great on you, too." Riselia smiled, examining Leonis and nodding in satisfaction.

And then, she slammed her fist into her palm, like she'd just come up with a good idea.

"Oh, right! Let's take a picture of Leo in this outfit!"

"Why didn't I think of that? Wait here, I'll go get the camera—" Regina made to take off.

"...Let's just go," Leonis said with a sigh. "Tessera is waiting for us."

◆

They took the shuttle bus to the orphanage, met up with Tessera, and then took another bus to Old Town. The evening sun was already dipping below the city walls, and a faint darkness was beginning to dye the sky. Like Leonis, Tessera was dressed in a child's yukata. Leonis thought it was a rented one, like his, but as it turned out, it was handmade by Phrenia.

They got off at the Sector Two station near Old Town and headed to the gate on foot. It was hard to walk in the wooden clogs, but apparently, they were part of the festival's atmosphere.

Naturally, there were far more people around than there had been two days ago. And since it was a day off, there were many students. Leonis recognized this because plenty of them were walking around in their uniforms.

"...I thought wearing yukatas was part of the rules here?" Leonis said, casting a suspicious glare in Riselia's direction.

"I—I wanted to see you in a yukata!" Riselia confessed, unable to look Leonis in the eye.

The main street was lit with mana lanterns, and the sounds of the festival musicians grew gradually louder. Many stalls were set up along the streets, giving the place a very different feel.

"There sure are a lot of people around here," Riselia remarked quietly.

"Yeah. We should take care not to get separated," Leonis said, offering Tessera his arm.

"Huh? L-Leo...? Um..." Tessera bashfully took his hand, her face flushing as she lowered her head. "Th-thank you..."

Riselia took his other hand. "Make sure you don't get lost, either, Leo."

"I'll be fine. I have my communication terminal with me."

"No," she chided firmly. "Some bad grown-up might decide to snatch you."

"...I doubt that."

Tessera giggled as she watched their exchange.

"Look at you, kid, so popular ♪," Regina teased, poking him on the back of his neck.

Leonis frowned. "S-stop that, please."

"Ah, look at that! It's so cute..." Riselia had stopped and was looking at one of the stalls.

If anything's cute here, it's you, Leonis thought for some reason. His minion's eyes were fixed on candied apples and mandarins. It was exactly the sort of sweet one might expect a girl to like.

"No, if anything's cute here, it's you, Lady Selia," Regina needled.

"...R-Regina, what are you saying?!"

◆

Arle Kirlesio perused the streets beneath the glow of the mana lanterns.

What a lively festival this is. Even though the world is being overrun by unknown monsters...

The excitement of this bright celebration was something she would never have known in her forest. Elves had their own festivals, of course, but they were much more austere and quiet affairs. Arle felt ill at ease in this crowd.

Why was she there, then? That was quite simple—the Dark Lord Zol Vadis had ordered the Demon Wolf Pack here to keep a watchful eye for terrorists that might attack.

When Lena told her of their mission, Arle had wanted to remind the dark elf that they were terrorists, too, but she managed to stop herself.

"I will admit the food stalls are nice, though..."

As she ate fried noodles she'd bought from one of the vendors, Arle looked around the area. An elf's sense of hearing was keen enough to pick up on conversations even in places packed with people.

But then, suddenly, her gaze settled on a girl dressed in white. She was strolling through the crowd like a ghost. Her hair was a vivid blue, and her face was concealed behind a mask. Perhaps she'd bought it at one of the stalls? It hardly made her inconspicuous, yet no one seemed aware of her presence.

That blue hair...

Arle immediately recalled the swordswoman she'd encountered at the pier a few days ago. Had her hair been so long, though?

...Why? Something about that girl feels...

Sensing something ominous from the masked young woman, Arle resolved to follow her.

...Huh?

Yet before she had the chance, the girl disappeared into the crowd.

◆

Leonis and his group went around the plaza, enjoying the cotton candy and candy apples they bought.

"Oh, there's a target shooting stall there. I'm good at that!" Regina said happily, tugging on Leonis's sleeve.

"I'd imagine you are," he replied.

"Can I try it, Lady Selia?"

Riselia nodded with a bit of a forced smile. "Go ahead..."

Apparently, this was a game where one was meant to knock down prizes with a toy gun.

"Which one do you want, Tessera?" Regina asked as she stuffed a cork bullet into the barrel.

"Umm. I want that...stuffed bear..."

"The stuffed bear? It's a bit large, but I'll get it for you!"

Regina closed an eye and held up the gun. Suddenly, her expression changed from a girl enjoying a festival to that of a sagacious sharpshooter.

"Anti-Large Aerial Beast Extermination Weapon—Dragon Slayer!" With that cry of enthusiasm, she pulled the trigger.

The cork bullet whizzed through the air and hit the stuffed bear right between the eyes—but the bear only wobbled in place.

"..."

"I hit it! I did!"

"Missy, hitting it isn't enough. You have to knock it down, too," the person managing the stall said with a grin.

"...Mm. Fine," Regina replied as she loaded the toy gun again. "How about this, then?!"

Pop! Pop!

She fired two shots, both of which struck the exact same spot seconds apart from each other. But once again, the stuffed toy only wobbled slightly.

"Regina, maybe you should just give up...," Riselia told her.

"Not yet, Lady Selia! I'll try to calculate the right angle this time—"

"Let me try," Leonis interjected, lowering her arms and taking the gun away.

"Kid..."

"Leo?"

The two girls looked at him curiously, but Leonis only nodded and loaded a cork bullet into the barrel. The stall keeper sneered at him.

Devil's bullet, gouge through fate itself...

He fired a shot charged with a bit of mana, which hit a can sitting on the edge of the shelf. A miss...at least normally. However, the bullet quickly rebounded, hitting a nearby prize. It wobbled, veered sideways, and hit the adjacent prize, and then the prize next to it, and the prize next to that, too. Eventually it hit the stall's pillar, deflected again, and hit the stuffed bear directly.

Like Regina's attempts, the bear didn't fall. The cork dropped to the ground, bounced, and shot toward the bear again. It repeated this twice, thrice, four times, five times, six. The miracle looped over and over, and the single-bullet barrage eventually knocked the bear off the shelf.

"Phew, that was a difficult shot," Leonis remarked with a shrug as he returned the toy gun.

"L-Leo, that was amazing...!" Tessera said, her eyes wide with respect and awe.

"N-not bad, kid...," Regina added, obviously amazed.

Riselia did notice he'd used sorcery but only cracked a smile, seemingly content to overlook it.

"Well, that's that. Now, let's collect the prize—"

"S-stop screwing with me!" the stall keeper bellowed at them. "That made no sense! You cheated!"

Tessera fearfully hid behind Leonis.

"If anyone's cheating, it's you," Leonis countered, pointing at the prize shelf.

There was a rod where the stuffed bear had been, and the toy had been caught on it, keeping it from falling.

"...Y-you brat!"

Angered at having his fraud exposed, the man grabbed Leonis by his yukata's collar.

Leonis sneered coldly. "Oho? So you wish to experience the terror of death..."

"Wh-what...?" the man replied, his face contorting in anger.

Suddenly, a sharp voice cut into their exchange.

"What are you doing? I ask that you refrain from resorting to violence."

Leonis turned around and saw a black-haired girl approaching.

"Miss Finé!" Riselia exclaimed happily.

Elfiné was moving through the crowd. She had the Executive Committee's band on her arm and was accompanied by two orbs.

"Miss Elfiné, what are you doing here?" Leonis asked.

"The Executive Committee asked me to help manage the festival," she explained. "I often get called to assist with security during events like this."

...*That makes sense.*

Her Eye of the Witch's power was quite useful for such large-scale celebrations. Long-distance communications, guiding refugees, finding lost children, watching suspicious figures, and...stopping brawls. Elfiné could cover quite the large area with all eight of her orbs active.

Of course, since Elfiné was only one person, she still needed the assistance of others to handle everything.

"So what's happening here? Why would you raise a hand to a child...?" Elfiné questioned, cocking an eyebrow.

"Ah, well... Hm..." The man hurriedly released Leonis.

"He was trying to cheat people out of their money," Leonis said, pointing at the shelf.

"...?" Elfiné followed his gaze and quickly realized what had happened.

"No, um, well...," the man fumbled.

"We'll hear what you have to say at headquarters. For now, your business is suspended," Elfiné stated, placing a sticker that declared as much on the stall's sign. "Thank you for your cooperation, everyone."

She bowed her head to Leonis and the rest of the group and left with the dejected man.

"Wow, Miss Finé looks busy," Riselia commented.

Regina nodded and replied, "I'd bet. Let's stop by headquarters later and bring her a snack from the festival."

"Here you go, Tessera." Leonis had picked up the plush bear and was handing it to the girl.

"Th-thank you, Leo!" Although blushing, the nine-year-old accepted it happily and hugged the bear tight.

◆

Leonis looked around, keeping his eyes out for any trouble. He and the others strolled down the main street toward where Sakuya's dance would be held.

Riselia pointed at a crowd that formed ahead. "Look over there. Did something happen?"

The people were cheering at something.

"It must be a street performance. Let's check it out," replied Regina.

"Good idea." Riselia turned to look at Tessera, who nodded in consent. Set in the middle of the ring of audience members was a large umbrella, with entertainers standing under it.

...Let's see how these performers match up to my skeleton circus, Leonis thought as he wove through the throng to get a better look.

"...?!"

Immediately, his expression tensed. There were two familiar faces performing.

A girl in a yukata stood under the umbrella, juggling daggers and balls skillfully, with a rather blank expression. And sitting by her side was a large black wolf, balancing a large ball on its nose.

...Shary and Blackas?!

As the audience showered them with applause, Leonis sent a telepathic message their way.

"What in the blasted hells are you two doing?!"

"Ah, my lord—" Shary turned her head, noticing Leonis's presence. *"You look very cute in that outfit, my lord!"*

"Grr...forget about me. Just what are you doing here?"

"We've concluded that this disguise will be most effective for blending in," Blackas replied while keeping the ball balanced on his nose.

"No, I'd say you stand out quite a bit."

"That is fine. We are, as they say, hiding in plain sight."

"...Hm. I see."

Blackas had a point. Rather than suspiciously clinging to the dark corners of the festival, operating where one wouldn't suspect could be more effective.

"And we get so many sweets, too!" Shary happily appended.

Set beneath them was a box, filled to the brim with assorted treats that onlookers had thrown in.

"...So that's what you were after."

"N-not at all, my lord! This is all in the name of camouflage—"

"Very well. Just report in if anything happens."

"W-we will...!"

Even as she communicated with Leonis, Shary didn't drop what she was juggling.

"That girl's amazing," Riselia praised as she clapped.

"Don't you think she looks kind of familiar, though, Lady Selia?" Regina asked.

"Now that you mention it, I feel like I've seen her somewhere before...," Riselia responded pensively.

"Y-you must be imagining things. Let's go!" Leonis insisted, pulling on the sleeve of Riselia's yukata.

"W-wait, Leo!"

They crossed a bridge over the river through the city, when suddenly—

Pop! Pop! Pop!

—Small explosions shook the air.

"...Get down!" Leonis turned around and called out sharply.

"Leo?" Riselia questioned as a few more blasts sounded in the sky.

"...That's...the sixth-order spell, Guren Zo?!"

"Leo, Leo...!" As he shielded the three girls with his back, Riselia rested a hand on his shoulder. "Those are fireworks."

"..." Leonis fell silent for a long moment, processing what she had just told him.

"Sakura Orchid fireworks are so pretty!" Regina cheered.

Pop, pop, pop pop pop.

The fireworks whistled as they took off, painting the sky with brilliant, flowerlike patterns of light.

"...I—I know what fireworks are, of course," Leonis stated, clearing his throat.

"Heh-heh, you were trying to protect us, weren't you, Leo?" Riselia giggled.

"N-no!"

"I think there's a better view over there, Lady Selia!" Regina pointed at a spot with fewer people.

Standing under an artificial tree meant to purify the water supply, Leonis gazed at the fireworks blooming across the sky for a bit. He'd relinquished the top of the tree to Tessera, so that she'd have a better view. It was tough to view much from where he was standing, though, even on his tiptoes.

"You can't see from there, can you, Leo?" Riselia said, placing her hands under his arms and picking him up.

"M-Miss Selia?! P-put me down!" Leonis protested, his face flushed and his limbs struggling in midair.

"Stop thrashing around, Leo. ♪"

Nearby people looked on, smiling and laughing at the heartwarming sight.

◆

The wavering flames of a campfire lit up the darkness. Sakuya sat in a silent room of the shrine. She had just finished purifying her body at the spring and donned her priestess garb. Before her was a wooden box containing an ancestral sword, a sacred treasure passed down in the Sakura Orchid's royal house.

"You look quite beautiful, Princess Sakuya," said Eika, who stood behind and was aiding with the preparations.

"I'm sure Setsura would be much prettier," Sakuya replied.

"It's almost time for the ritual. Make sure you're ready."

"All right."

Sakuya picked up the wooden box containing the sword and moved to the altar. This was a hallowed custom that none were permitted to intrude upon. Doing so was an unforgivable taboo.

The ritual was meant to offer the blood of a priestess to Raijinki, who slumbered within the city's Mana Furnace. The dance Sakuya would perform before the people was to be done after that.

She hadn't heard from the Kenki Gathering since the afternoon she'd spent with Leonis. But they were undoubtedly hidden somewhere in the city, biding their time. They couldn't have much

time left. The power of emptiness consumed the souls of those who wielded Demon Swords.

...The Kenki Gathering. They seek a place to die as warriors...

There was a good chance they'd try something during the climax of the ritual. Sakuya didn't know how they'd accomplish it, but their aim was to awaken Raijinki and use the god to lure out the Void Lord who had destroyed the Sakura Orchid.

Only a priestess—only I can release Raijinki, though.

Sakuya slowed to a stop. Sitting on ground covered with white sand was a large rock, severed in two. This was the divine rock—the altar—that had been taken from the Sakura Orchid's ruined capital.

The young woman placed the wooden crate containing the sacred treasure before the altar. She then opened the crate and retrieved the sword. After pricking herself with it, she would drip blood on the stone.

However, right as she picked up the blade...

"...?!"

Sakuya froze up, sensing a faint presence. Looking around, she spotted a ghostly figure amid the sea of white sand. It was a masked girl, clad in white Sakura Orchid attire. Her long blue hair trailed in the breeze, faintly illuminated by the flames of the bonfire.

"...Who are you?" Sakuya demanded sharply.

No normal girl could enter this place. Raiou had Murakumo operatives set up a perimeter around the shrine. Not even an ant could get here undetected.

The figure didn't answer, but stepped forward and summoned a katana to her hand.

A moment later, steel flashed in the dark.

◆

Countless beautiful lights illuminated the sky, casting shadows on the ground below. The Kenki Gathering stood unseen, clad in their anti-Void protection suits, patiently awaiting the appointed time.

"The hour is upon us. We will have our revenge."

All thirty-seven Demon Swordsmen glared into the emptiness, each one willing to lay down their life if it meant vanquishing the Void Lord who had destroyed their homeland.

Sacrificing the innocents of the Seventh Assault Garden to see their wish fulfilled didn't trouble them in the slightest. They'd already steeled their resolve the moment they corrupted the Holy Swords granted to them by the planet and turned them into Demon Swords.

I do regret that we couldn't bring Princess Sakuya over to our side.

She had rejected the hand Uzan had extended to her and would suffer the consequences.

Just then...

"—Hello, Uzan. The operation is going smoothly, I hope?"

"...?"

Hearing an odd, out-of-place voice come from his communication terminal, Uzan frowned beneath his vision. It was Finzel Phillet, the Kenki Gathering's employer.

"Oh, it's you. We're on an important operation. Keep communications to a mini—"

"Now, now, just hear me out. Think of this as my farewell to you."

"What do you want?"

As their sponsor, Finzel was the one who'd provided them with the anti-Void protection suits, an infiltration plan into the Seventh Assault Garden, a hiding place...and even their Demon Swords. Finzel was a true blessing for the Kenki Gathering.

Of course, there were some within the group who regarded this overly generous benefactor with suspicion, but they quickly rescinded all criticism when he brought a certain girl to them. It was Princess Setsura. Their sovereign, who had died the same day as their homeland.

"Look, we're grateful to you for granting us a place to die and a chance at revenge."

"**Hmm, I see. Sorry, but I have to ask you to repay that debt of gratitude to me now.**"

"You can be sure that we will. Although we may not be fighting for your... What was it called again? Your...Demon Sword Project? It needs our combat data. And we promise we will go all out today to provide for you."

"**That's very encouraging to hear. But see, I'm something of a perfectionist, so I set up a little trick to make sure you put forth your best effort, gentlemen.**"

"...What?"

The next moment, the information terminal in Uzan's suit lit up, and a small, winged fairy, small enough to sit in the palm of one's hand, flew out of it. The glowing fairy flapped its wings, as black as those of a swallowtail butterfly, as it darted through the air.

"Lord Phillet, what is this...?"

"**The Artificial Elemental Seraphim. A messenger capable of conveying the goddess's voice with its whispers. I used the Astral Garden's network to sneak it into the protector suits you're all wearing.**"

"What...? What is the meaning of this?!"

"**You'll have to forgive me. Your Demon Swords will be a sacrifice for the second coming of the goddess.**"

And then, the fairy, the goddess's oracle, whispered words of the future—

"...A-ahhhh... Ahhhhhhhhhhhhhhhhhhhhhhhhhh!"

The Kenki Gathering's protection suits all shattered...

And from their wreckage emerged thirty-seven Void monsters.

CHAPTER 8

SETSURA

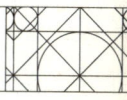

She's quick...!

Skrrrrrrrrrrrrrrrrrrrrrrr!

The first slash Sakuya blocked made that evident. The girl she was facing was much stronger than she was. In terms of sheer sword skills, even Sakuya's upperclassmen were no match for her, yet this masked girl...

...She's got me on the ropes!

Their blades clashed, spitting sparks. Sakuya exhaled hard and kicked off the ground to leap away and distance herself from her opponent. The masked girl didn't pursue and simply lowered her katana offhandedly. Despite meeting Raikirimaru, the masked girl's weapon wasn't so much as nicked. That shouldn't have been possible for an ordinary weapon.

...A Holy Swordswoman...

It wasn't clear yet what power this enemy commanded, but Sakuya couldn't sense the ominous aura of a Demon Sword about her.

"Are you with the Kenki Gathering?" Sakuya demanded, tightening her grip on Raikirimaru.

"..."

The masked girl neither confirmed nor denied anything. She only raised her Holy Sword again. Strained silence fell over the two. The sounds of their fight hadn't drawn anyone's attention, and no one was coming to help.

That struck Sakuya as strange. Yes, the shrine was closed off, but surely Eika and the other guards would have heard their clash and come over by now. When Sakuya looked around, she recognized that the scenery was off.

She narrowed her eyes. On closer inspection, the air over the trees wavered like heat haze.

...A barrier of some kind. This must be her Holy Sword's ability.

It must have prevented all sound within from escaping.

"You've clearly come here prepared. What are you after?!"

Even if this girl was an operative of the Kenki Gathering, she didn't seem to be working toward the same goal as the others. The Kenki Gathering sought to release the Sakura Orchid god sealed in the Mana Furnace, using it to summon the Void Lord they wanted dead. Killing the priestess, Sakuya, was entirely at odds with that.

The Kenki Gathering did mention they had a princess priestess of their own... Is this her?!

The masked girl took half a step forward.

Here she comes!

Sakuya activated Raikirimaru's acceleration power. White plasma crackled as Sakuya vanished.

"Mikagami-style swordsmanship—Thundering Lightning Slash!"

Several slashes flashed through the dark of the night. This was a blade technique meant for countering large Voids. A shower of cuts, as elusive as smoke, rained down on the masked girl.

...Yet Sakuya didn't feel any of them land. Her opponent's visage faded away like mist.

"...?!"

On instinct, Sakuya whirled and raised her electrified Holy Sword.

Skriiiiiiiiiiiiiii!

There came an earsplitting, dissonant noise. She was able to deflect the attack, but...

"—Demonic wind!"

An invisible surge of air issued from her opponent's blade, knocking Sakuya's body away. Her back hit the ground hard, forcing the breath from her lungs.

"Ngah...!"

The masked girl brought down her Holy Sword, and the sand on the ground around her scattered... Not a moment later, something invisible and sharp bit into the shoulder of Sakuya's priestess outfit.

"...That Holy Sword... It uses the power of the wind!" Sakuya said through gritted teeth while holding her bleeding shoulder.

Both the afterimage that remained as the masked girl dodged Sakuya's attack and the unseen cut at her shoulder had been air-based Holy Sword powers. The same was likely true of the barrier.

No good...!

Loath though she was to admit it, Sakuya understood from the brief fight that her enemy was stronger than her.

"...You're not an opponent I can afford to hold back against," Sakuya muttered, turning Raikirimaru's blade.

Void miasma began seeping from her right arm.

"Demon Sword—Yamichidori."

A black mist enveloped her Holy Sword, and it began to shine

with a dark, otherworldly glow. Black lightning crackled, charring the ground.

"...Oh?" The masked girl spoke for the first time. Her voice sounded younger than Sakuya had imagined. "Why do you have a Demon Sword?"

Ignoring her words, Sakuya sped forward and swung Yamichidori down. The blade of wind met with the dark sword, loosing a violent burst of air.

"Ahhhhhhhhhhhhhhhhhhhhhh!"

This time, however, Sakuya wasn't overpowered. She pushed harder, and then...

Crack...!

A fissure ran across the girl's mask.

"...?!"

The white thing shattered, falling away with a sound like broken ceramics. Long blue locks billowed in the gusts emanating from the girl's katana. The face of Sakuya's enemy was unmistakable.

"Setsu...ra...?"

Sakuya's eyes went wide.

◆

At first, Leonis thought it was just the sounds of the fireworks. But a moment later, a pillar of intense fire erupted with a thundering noise.

"...What?!" Riselia shouted sharply as she stood to shield Leonis and Tessera.

Boom, boom, booooooooom!

A series of intermittent explosions shook the air. Old Town's buildings began to collapse one after another, and the crowd screamed in terror.

...Just what is going on?! Leonis wondered, startled.

"Lady Selia, look!" Regina called, pointing at the epicenter of one of the blasts.

Eerie figures were moving sluggishly within the burning flames. From a distance, they resembled large humanoids, standing five meters tall.

"...It can't be! Voids?!"

"But there were no signs of a Void outbreak...," Regina said, biting her lips.

Normally, when Voids appeared, they emerged from cracks that formed in midair. Excalibur Academy had constructed a system that could detect the subtle distortions in space caused by those fissures and trigger an alarm.

Yet this time, there were no such fractures in reality.

"—lia... Selia, can you hear me—" a voice issued from Riselia's terminal.

"Ah, Miss Finé!"

"Voids have appeared around Old Town—you confirm—?" Elfiné's voice was audibly stressed. Only pieces of her message came through because of the Voids' mana interference.

"Is this a Stampede...?"

"No, it isn't," Elfiné stated. **"This is only a small colony. I can't detect a Void Lord."**

"Do we know how large the group is and what class and rank the Voids are?"

"There's thirty to forty of them, meaning they're a squadron-sized colony. Each Void's estimated rank is... unknown. They don't match any kind recorded in the academy's data."

"Roger that. Given how destructive they are, I have to think they're at least B rank," Riselia answered, watching the plume of black smoke in the sky. "We'll move out to guide the citizens to safety. Please provide us with any updates you can."

"We're counting on you. I've got my orbs flying around, so set up a data link with them."

"Understood."

The transmission cut off, and Riselia turned to Regina and Leonis.

"You heard her. Let's do our duty as Holy Swordsmen."

"Yes, Lady Selia!"

Leonis nodded. "Okay."

"Protecting and guiding the citizens to safety is our top priority until reinforcements from Excalibur Academy arrive," Riselia instructed. "Regina, you take up position on elevated ground and shoot covering fire in every direction."

"Understood!" Regina moved out at once. "Holy Sword, Drag Striker! Activate!"

With her Holy Sword in its hunting rifle configuration, she made her way toward a nearby building.

"For the time being, I'll guard these people and make way for the shelter. Tessera, you come with me," Riselia said.

With a brave look on her face, Tessera replied, "O-okay!"

She knew better than to cry or throw a tantrum now. Undoubtedly she trusted Riselia and Leonis wholeheartedly.

Even so, she's something. Such grit from a nine-year-old... Leonis thought, rather impressed.

"Leo, you come with me, too..." Riselia trailed off, and her expression suddenly tensed. "Wait. I can't get in touch with Sakuya. Is it Void disruption? Or maybe it's the shrine's barrier..."

As the commander on the scene, Riselia surely wanted Sakuya, an ace Void slayer, fighting on the front lines. Although Sakuya wasn't the type to sit idle while the enemy was at their door, her knowledge of the situation would be limited if she didn't link up with the rest of the eighteenth platoon.

"—I'll go look for her," Leonis declared.

"Leo..."

"I'll find Miss Sakuya and handle the Voids on the other side of the bridge."

"All right. I'm counting on you," Riselia agreed. Then she directed her attention to the terrified citizens and spoke in a loud, dignified voice. "I am Riselia Crystalia, a Holy Swordswoman from Excalibur Academy! I will guide you to the shelter, so please stay calm and follow me!"

◆

"...I should hurry," Leonis muttered as he made a break for the forest that surrounded the shrine.

I assume those remnants of the Sakura Orchid must have done something...

There was a chance they were after Sakuya.

"—You have a grasp on the situation, yes, Shary?" Leonis asked.

"Yes, my lord." Shary's response reached his mind.

"This is my kingdom. I will not tolerate the loss of even a single one of my subjects."

"Understood, my lord."

Leonis summoned the Three Champions of Rognas from his shadow.

"Amilas, Dorug, and Nefisgal, you are to spread out and focus on guarding the underground shelters."

"—By your will!" The ancient warriors kneeled before Leonis and spoke as one.

"However, make sure not to stand out too much. Should there

be any major changes in the situation...do as Riselia Crystalia commands."

"Yes!"

"By your will!"

"I will redeem myself after my recent failure!"

"Good. I trust you to handle this," Leonis stated.

The undead champions silently jumped away and began bounding across the rooftops.

"Blackas, are you there?"

"—I am, Lord Magnus."

Leonis looked in the direction of the reply and spotted the black wolf standing atop a nearby roof. Leonis hastened to his friend and got on his back.

"We must get to Sakuya in the shrine. Hurry."

"Of course," Blackas said, preparing to take off at a sprint.

"Wait." Leonis retrieved a mask from his shadow. "Things might get troublesome if people recognize me."

He donned the mask, and darkness enveloped his yukata, morphing his visage into that of a Dark Lord.

"—Is it time for the elusive Dark Lord to take the stage?" Blackas asked him.

"Indeed. Now all shall know what Dark Lords are capable of."

◆

"I-it can't... It can't be..." Sakuya whispered. Her voice was trembling, and her face had gone pale.

This couldn't be real. It had to be a trick.

"I saw Setsura die... She was killed...right before my eyes..."

Sakuya felt the strength leave her body. Only her warrior instincts kept her from dropping Yamichidori. Her enemy's face was identical to her own, save the color of the eyes, which were a malevolent red, like that terrible star. As her blue locks billowed in the wind, she attacked.

Even when she was battling her younger sibling, Setsura's expression didn't betray any hint of emotion. She advanced on Sakuya, devoid even of bloodlust.

"Do you have a problem with my face?" she asked.

"...?!"

When Sakuya heard those words, determination began to swell in her heart.

This isn't Setsura.

It was only a monster wearing her face.

"Ahhhhhhhhhhhhhhhh!"

Void miasma poured out from Sakuya's body. Grass wilted, and trees grew dry and bare at its touch. Sakuya could tell she'd lost control, but there was no helping it.

She had to cut this thing down. She had to.

...It feels like I'm going to go mad!

Planting a foot powerfully on the ground, she leaped forward.

"Thunderflash Flurry!"

Yamichidori came racing down with the force of Sakuya's grief behind it. Pitch-black lightning crackled and surged.

Screeeeeeeeeech!

Demonic wind cried out, and the *thing* wearing her sister's face blocked the attack with ease.

"Who are you?! My sister is—" Sakuya took another step and struck again with all her might. Once more, her lightning was deflected, scattering plasma all around.

"Fascinating. It's consumed you so much already, so why haven't you succumbed to the emptiness...?"

"Shut up! How dare you talk to me with her face—with her voice! Mikagami-style swordsmanship—Sakura Petal Blizzard!"

Steel flashed countless times in the dark. Every swipe was aimed at the imposter, but Sakuya didn't feel like any connected.

She'd only managed to hit an afterimage formed by the Demon Sword controlling the wind. Detecting someone behind her, Sakuya spun around to attack.

Yamichidori had no scabbard, but by releasing the magnetic power contained in the weapon, she could reproduce a quick-draw-style attack.

"Lightning Slayer!"

The tip of her blade just barely nicked the girl's forehead.

It can't be... How did she dodge my Lightning Slayer?!

The Lightning Slayer was a finishing move. One delivered faster than human perception could follow. However, it left Sakuya wide open after executing it.

"Mikagami-style swordsmanship—Demonic Gale Slash."

As Sakuya stood there, stunned and out of position, the girl bore down on her. A katana wreathed in sinister wind cut through the young woman countless times, tearing her apart.

◆

"The shelter is this way! Hurry!" Riselia was leading civilians into the open safe area. Noticing Tessera's concern, she reassured the girl, "Don't worry! We'll keep this place safe!"

"O-okay! Be careful!" Tessera nodded and stayed behind as Riselia hurried off.

"—■■■■■■■!"

The Voids howled as grotesque arms sprouted from all over their bodies.

"Holy Sword, Bloody Sword—Activate!" Riselia called.

In response, particles of light issued from her hands, forming a beautiful sword. She brought the shining crimson tip of the blade to her arm, gently pricking it and allowing her blood to drip to the floor. The puddle of crimson around her formed multiple blades. Whistling as they moved, the liquid swords tore at her outfit. The cuffs and sleeves of her yukata went flying and fluttered to the ground in tattered bits.

"This should make it easier to move...," Riselia said, her eyes glinting with mana as she undid her hair.

...Here they come!

A hulking humanlike Void approached. Its appearance suggested it might be a subspecies of the ogre class. She didn't know what rank it was, but given how quickly it had smashed through buildings, it no doubt boasted impressive combat abilities.

Six months ago, Riselia wouldn't have been able to face this monster. Yet now she felt no fear.

It's all thanks to Leo training with me every day!

The six-armed Void howled as it charged toward her. Using the tip of her blade, Riselia drew a magic circle at her feet.

"Come forth, hunter of shadows, servant to the queen—" She intoned an ancient incantation.

It was a second-order necromancy spell—Grava Rajian, Shadow Wolf Summon.

Three shadowy beasts emerged from the shining array.

"Slow its legs!" Riselia swung her sword down, and the wolves pounced on the Void.

No sooner had they done so than the Vampire Queen ran forward herself.

"Kuh... Aaah..."

The pain nearly robbed her of consciousness. Her priestess garb was stained with blood, and she couldn't lift her arms. Her stiff fingers refused to budge, and her left eye had been blinded.

The burning pain was torturous agony.

"...Aaagh... Guh, aaah...," Sakuya choked out.

"So you used your Demon Sword to block the killing move. Impressive," a voice remarked.

Footsteps were growing louder.

...Have to...get up...

Gathering up every bit of willpower she had left, Sakuya bade her body to get up. And yet her limbs refused. She remained crouched in a puddle of blood, looking down on herself with her one functioning eye. Deep lacerations ran across her skin. Had Sakuya not guarded with Yamichidori, she would have died instantly. The injuries she'd sustained were far from nonlethal, however.

"Wh-why...?!" Sakuya breathed, lips quivering and dripping red.

Demonic Gale Slash was a technique passed down in the Mikagami royal house. How could this girl know it?

The answer was self-evident, but Sakuya refused to admit it.

It can't be her. This can't be Setsura...!

Then the girl kneeled before the helpless Sakuya and raised a hand. She caressed Sakuya's cheek with a finger, wiped the blood from it, and brought it to her mouth.

"...What are you...doing?!"

"—Drawing the blood of a priestess," the girl replied as she got to her feet and approached the stone altar. She then picked up the treasured sword, nicked her wrist on its edge, and splashed crimson on the altar.

"—Soul of the sealed god, abide by the ancient pact and awaken here."

A blue light shone from the rock. The blinding glow washed away the night as surely as the midday sun.

"S-stop... Stop it... Sister!" Sakuya cried.

She knew what this meant, for she'd seen it happen nine years ago. Two priestesses were awakening the Twin Gods of the Sakura Orchid.

Before long, the light died down, and darkness settled in again. The girl with the same face as her sister turned back to Sakuya.

"The hero of nothingness will surely come in search of the other god now..."

Was Sakuya about to die at the hands of her sibling? Even if Setsura didn't finish the job, Sakuya could feel her time growing short. There was no strength remaining in her body, and the Demon Sword in her grip dissolved into black mist and disappeared.

Icy fingers closed around Sakuya's neck. A face nearly identical to Sakuya's own stared into the younger girl's eyes.

"...Setsu...ra...," Sakuya croaked.

"I won't kill you. You're a valuable Demon Sword wielder. It'd be much better if you became a servant of my master."

"Ser...vant...?"

What was she saying? At this point, it didn't matter. That doubt was fading away along with everything else...

"—Gerz Zok!"

A shower of dark blades poured down from somewhere unseen.

"...?!"

Setsura released her sister and leaped away.

Although the words were unfamiliar, Sakuya recognized the voice.

...It can't be!

Through her remaining eye, she saw him, standing there with his arms crossed.

"—You have nerve, laying hands upon that which is mine without my permission."

It was the Dark Lord Zol Vadis.

◆

"The Dark...Lord...!" Sakuya's dry lips mouthed the words, even as her awareness flickered.

Why is he here...?!

Zol Vadis landed on the ground and addressed Setsura. "Were you the one who beckoned the Voids here?"

"..."

Silence. Setsura faced the Dark Lord while keeping a cautious distance from him.

"You refuse to answer a Dark Lord's question? Insolent fool."

Zol Vadis produced six fireballs in his hand, casting light all around.

"What...?!" he exclaimed upon glimpsing the face of the enemy. "Sakuya...?! No, you're..."

Seizing upon the Dark Lord's confusion, Setsura attacked with a horizontal cut of her Holy Sword. Demonic wind surged toward Zol Vadis.

He was not the actual target, however. Setsura's real aim was Sakuya, who lay beside the Dark Lord.

"Tsk... Li Ralute!"

With a flap of his mantle, the Dark Lord conjured a barrier that stopped the deadly gale.

Whooooooooooooooosh!

The wind raged, felling the nearby trees and kicking up a cloud of dust.

"She ran off...," the Dark Lord muttered.

Setsura was nowhere to be found.

Zol Vadis directed his attention to the young woman at his feet. "Sakuya Sieglinde, who was that? Why is her face the same as yours?"

"...That's what I want to know," Sakuya just barely managed to reply. "Maybe a ghost..."

"Ghosts are low-grade undead. She didn't look that weak to me." The Dark Lord whispered something Sakuya didn't quite understand.

"Why did you save me? I...turned down your deal..."

"I merely came to punish that fool for laying hands on that which is mine."

"I don't recall...ever agreeing to become yours...," Sakuya answered weakly, cracking a wry smile.

"In time, this entire kingdom will belong to me...," the Dark Lord stated, then he kneeled into the puddle. "At this rate, you will die."

"...Yes...I know..."

"Regrettably, I'm not capable of healing sorcery..." Zol Vadis shook his head. "However, princess of the Sakura Orchid, in honor of the courage you demonstrated in my castle, I will give you one more chance to negotiate with me."

"...Wh-what?" Sakuya's working eye widened.

"—I bid you open, lock of the Realm of Shadows," the Dark Lord chanted, holding up his right hand.

Countless sparkling jewels appeared in his palm.

No...they're not gems, Sakuya realized. The little spheres that glittered with colorful light were...

"These are mystic eyes."

"Eyes...?"

"A collection of mystic eyes is the symbol of a powerful Dark Lord. We then offer them as rewards to subordinates who have made impressive accomplishments on the field of battle."

Sakuya was struck by a feeling that Zol Vadis was grinning beneath his mask.

"They come from many sources. Demons, divine beasts, half-god heroes, devils, demi-gods, and even dragons. The mystic eyes of beasts. The mystic eyes of petrification. The mystic eyes of ruination. The mystic eyes of the hawk, of the divine, of time. Mystic eyes to break magic, to gaze into truth, to read into souls..."

The tiny orbs glittered in midair like a replica of the starry sky.

"...What are you...trying to do?" Sakuya questioned.

"I will implant one of these in place of your lost left eye. Once the mystic eye links with your nerves, it will repair the damage done to your body."

"...That's...rather generous of you."

"No, not at all," the Dark Lord admitted. "Taking in a mystic eye means you will discard your humanity. Depending on which you choose, you will become a half-devil, a half-dragon, or something else entirely."

"..."

"Make your choice, princess of the Sakura Orchid. Will you bravely embrace your demise, or accept the power I offer and serve the Dark Lord Zol Vadis?"

"...That's a stupid question...Dark Lord." Sakuya smirked. "I don't need to think twice about this."

"...Oh?"

The faces of her companions in the eighteenth platoon surfaced in Sakuya's mind. Riselia, Regina, Elfiné, and Leonis—her fellow Holy Swordsmen, who'd sworn to fight the Voids alongside her. And then...her sister.

...I can't afford to die here.

Drawing on all the power she had left, Sakuya extended a hand.

"Dark Lord Zol Vadis. I accept your offer."

"...I see." The Dark Lord nodded. "What power do you wish for in return?"

"Speed," Sakuya replied unflinchingly. "I want a speed she will never be able to catch—to move faster than lightning."

"...Very well, then. Then I bequeath this mystic eye upon you." The Dark Lord picked one of the eyes floating in the air and handed it to her. "The mystic eye of time that I stole from the Temporal Devil..."

Sakuya pressed the mystic eye to her own ruined one, and then...

"...Aaah... Ugh, ahhhhhhhhhhhhhhhhhhhhhhhhhh!"

It burned. It ached. It seethed. It blazed. It throbbed. It stung. All manners of agony coursed through her. Then there was a light. Something foreign invaded her body. It was torturous. Like something had latched on to her soul and was stirring it up.

"I'm sorry, Miss Sakuya. Bear with it... Just a little longer."

From somewhere distant, a familiar boy's voice called to her, but...

"Ahhhhhhhhhhhhhhhhhhhhhhhhhhhhhhhhhhhhh!"

Sakuya's consciousness cut off right then and there.

◆

"It seemed her body didn't reject the eye," Leonis remarked as he gently set an unconscious Sakuya down on the ground.

Her wounds were beginning to heal. Riselia had died instantly, so he'd no choice but to make her an undead minion. Fortunately, Sakuya had evaded fatal injury. That said, if he'd left her as she was, she would've perished before long.

...And turning her into an undead would've been too great a risk.

Leonis's death sorcery worked in accordance with the compatibility of the target's soul. Riselia being made a Vampire Queen was nothing short of a miracle.

"Still, who was that other Sakuya...?"

Leonis scanned the area and then discovered something on the ground. A white mask had been split in two.

Isn't this...? Leonis thought as he retrieved the pieces.

"What's wrong, Lord Magnus?" Blackas inquired, emerging from the dancing shadows cast by the bonfire.

He'd remained hidden to keep his alliance with the Dark Lord from Sakuya.

"This mask. It belongs to the assassin who disposed of Zemein in Necrozoa."

"...Hm. Are you certain?"

"Positive. I think the assassin wore some manner of white garb, although I can't quite remember. I'll have to confirm it with Shary later." Leonis stowed the mask in his shadow. "The one who silenced Zemein, eh...?"

Between this and the Voids that appeared in Old Town, it looked more and more like the former lieutenants of the Dark Lords' Armies were behind the incident with the Sakura Orchid mercenaries.

"...They're like bothersome flies," Leonis spat bitterly.

Blackas nodded. "Agreed."

The ground under them suddenly rumbled.

"...A mega-float of this size, shaking?" Leonis turned and saw that a shining, blinding light had appeared above the Seventh Assault Garden. "Is that... Did the Sakura Orchid's god awaken?"

The god of the Sakura Orchid was fused with the Seventh Assault Garden's Mana Furnace, and the light was concentrated over the Central Garden.

Leonis looked at the stone altar, which was now stained with blood. It seemed that the girl who shared Sakuya's face had performed the ritual to unleash the god.

"Even if Sakuya were to awaken, I don't think she'd be able to simply reseal it."

According to her, that Sakura Orchid group was plotting something that would bring about the destruction of the city. Leonis didn't know what their next move was, but...

"God or not, I can't let anyone go rampaging through my kingdom..." Leonis sighed and drew the Staff of Sealed Sins from his shadow.

CHAPTER 9

THE MIGHTIEST SWORDMASTER

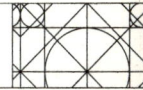

Shardark Void Lord.

The nothingness in the form of a one-eyed swordsman brought his greatsword down on Sakuya's head. The young girl squeezed her eyes shut, bracing herself for what was to come.

Yet the moment before the end, the Void Lord froze—because of something he saw behind Sakuya.

"...You. Why have you appeared here...?"

<I traced the thread of causality to glimpse this fate,> said a voice so garbled with static that it was hard to discern if it belonged to a man or a woman.

Sakuya turned around and saw a large mass of shadow that writhed formlessly.

...What?!

The voice then spoke again, as if it had read Sakuya's heart.

<I am the future. Or perhaps past. Or perhaps causality. The emptiness. Destiny itself...>

The darkness extended a shapeless arm, touched Sakuya's forehead, and then...

<—You who have been guided by causality. If you seek power, accept the emptiness.>

"...?!"

Oddly enough, Sakuya felt no fear, only hatred for the Void that had brought ruin to the Sakura Orchid, consumed Fuujinki, and killed her sister.

And so she accepted it.

"Ahhhhhh, ahhhhhhhhhhhhhhhhhhhh!"

"What?!"

She thought she could hear the Void Lord gasp. The six-year-old child was swallowed in a black miasma, and a katana crackling with dark lightning manifested in her hand.

"...!"

Crying out, Sakuya swung her newly formed Demon Sword at the Void Lord's heart!

Crack...

A noise like fracturing glass sounded.

Crack... Crack, crack, crack...!

"...?!"

The Void Lord's body—or more accurately, the space it occupied—splintered, and the one-eyed man vanished into the gap.

"...It's time. A pity, but no doubt you already predicted this," Shardark whispered spitefully.

His gaze was fixed not on Sakuya, who had stabbed him, but at the dark mass behind her.

"Hear me, goddess. Someday I shall reach you. I will cross all fate and all causality, so my blade will finally claim your head...!"

With that, Shardark Void Lord vanished before Sakuya's eyes—sinking into the crack in space.

◆

"...Ugh... Kuh!"

Caught in the throes of burning agony, Sakuya awakened. The back of her left eye throbbed faintly.

A memory...only...a memory...

Lying alone in the night, Sakuya put a hand over her left eye. The moment she'd accepted the mystic eye, an odd sensation had overcome her, as if past and future had bent backward to connect.

The sensation may have driven her to insanity had she not passed out.

...He called it the mystic eye of a Temporal Devil.

Sitting up, Sakuya slowly pulled her palm away. Her body moved effortlessly, and her injuries had mended.

No, this is...

They hadn't healed on their own; they'd been fixed. When the mystic eye linked with her, it forcibly stitched all the wounds in her body shut.

Just what happened to me?

When Sakuya tried to stand, she was assailed by a bizarre feeling akin to vertigo. The world seemed to double or triple itself.

What's going on... Is this eye defective...? She would've complained to the Dark Lord, but he was already gone. *I suppose I should be grateful enough that he saved my life...*

Sakuya looked at Old Town. Pillars of fire were rising from every street. Farther beyond, in the skies over the Central Garden, a bright light shone down like the sun.

Sakuya recognized it from that day nine years ago.

Raijinki's been unleashed...

Once a god had been released, sealing it again wasn't easy. During the attack on the Sakura Orchid, in the few hours the Void Lord spent fusing with Fuujinki, Sakuya and Setsura had to work together to shut Raijinki away. And since this wasn't Sakura

Orchid land, Sakuya didn't think she could manage to return the deity to the Seventh Assault Garden's Mana Furnace on her own.

"Sister..."

Had that truly been Setsura? She'd used the Mikagami style, just like Sakuya did, and had set Raijinki loose.

...Did she rise from the grave somehow?

The capital wasn't aware of any Holy Swords that could resurrect the dead, but a Demon Sword might have possessed such a power.

But if it's really her, what's she after...?

Did Setsura simply desire revenge on the Void Lord, like the Kenki Gathering? Unleashing Raijinki was only the first step in their plan. The god was bait for Shardark Void Lord, the actual target.

...She had to stop them. Whether the Kenki Gathering could defeat the Void Lord didn't matter. The resulting Stampede would claim the lives of many innocent civilians either way.

"I have to do something..."

Explosions rocked Old Town, and flames danced on the streets.

...The eighteenth platoon should be helping out there.

If so, then Old Town was in good hands. The more pressing matter was Raijinki, who had appeared above the Central Garden. The Dark Lord Zol Vadis was likely heading to confront the deity.

I'm not sure if I'll be of any use, but...

If the Dark Lord weakened Raijinki, Sakuya had a chance at resealing the god.

"Holy Sword... Activate!" Sakuya reached her hand out and summoned her Holy Sword.

If I use Raikirimaru's acceleration power, I can get there in time...

Then, the young woman saw her face reflected in the katana's polished blade. Her left eye gave off an amber glow.

"This is...!"

Once again, a sense of vertigo washed over her. Three disparate images of the world were overlapping, and a flood of information poured into her mind.

"Kuh, aaah... Guh...!"

Feeling as if the nerves in her left eye might burst, Sakuya gripped her head.

What was...that...?

As she clenched her teeth from the pain, Sakuya steadied her breathing. When she opened her eye, the overlaid world was one.

This is a mystic eye of time... Did I just gaze into the possibilities of the future...?

A mystic eye that allowed one to peer into possible outcomes. And Sakuya had just witnessed one potential branch. In it, she glimpsed the devastation brought by the Voids—and at its center was a girl in white.

"...Sister...!"

◆

Kzzzzzzzzzzzzzzzzzzzzzzzzzzzzzzzzzzzzzzzt!

A gigantic figure hurled spears of lightning that pierced the Central Garden's high-rise buildings. The lights in the city went out, accompanied by rolling thunder.

"So it's a devil," remarked Leonis. He was on a rooftop, seated on Blackas's back.

For it to be worshipped as a god, it had to be an incredibly powerful demon.

"It must have served the Luminous Powers and been degraded to a local god of the land when it lost its masters," Leonis concluded.

"Do we destroy it?" Blackas asked.

"Hm..." Leonis contemplated the question.

With his seal undone, Raijinki was on a rampage. And since it had been used to provide energy for the Mana Furnace, its divinity as a guardian deity had likely diminished. Still, if it wasn't brought under control, its destruction would extend beyond the Central Garden and reach Excalibur Academy.

Leonis sneered beneath his mask. "Defeating a mere devil will be easy, but it's the heart of the Mana Furnace. I'd rather not destroy it outright."

He had plans to build a mobile fortress for his Dark Lords' Armies, one that would match humanity's Assault Gardens. Necrozoa's Death Hold had been stationary, and honestly, he'd always envied Veira's Azure Hold and Azra-Ael's Otherworldly Castle.

"You might want to reconsider, Lord Magnus," Blackas cautioned.

"What?"

The black wolf turned his head up. "Look at that."

—*Crack... Crack... Crack...!*

Fissures began forming in the sky around Raijinki.

"...So the Voids are already coming."

Based on what Sakuya had told Leonis, the Kenki Gathering wanted to use Raijinki to get the attention of the Void Lord who had destroyed their home. Leonis had hoped to trap the deity in the Realm of Shadows before that happened, but...

"We have no choice. We must destroy the Sakura Orchid god before the Voids emerge," Leonis declared, dismounting Blackas.

He then tapped the bottom of the Staff of Sealed Sins on the floor.

"Perish, minion of the gods—Meld Gaiez!"

The tenth-order destruction spell activated, and a blast of intense darkness swallowed the lightning devil.

"...Hmph, pathetic."

"Lord Magnus!" Blackas called out sharply.

A bolt lanced from the smoke of the explosion, racing toward Leonis.

"...Rua Meires!" Leonis reflexively thrust his hand forward and chanted another spell.

A force field manifested in front of his palm, deflecting the lightning bolt.

"Tch. If I had my proper amount of mana, that spell would have slain it at once," Leonis remarked bitterly.

In this troublesome human body, his power was roughly a third of what it had been.

"Very well, I'll simply destroy you with my next attack...!" Leonis said, and he began to incite a second Meld Gaiez, this time using the Staff of Sealed Sins to boost the magic's power. "Perish!"

Boooooooooooooooooooom!

A deafening blast rang out as a dark flash once again shook the sky. Even a devil couldn't have survived that.

"...I might have done wrong by Sakuya."

Although he'd had no other option, he was still killing the Sakura Orchid's guardian.

—*Crack...*

A tear formed at the epicenter of the explosion.

Crack, crack, crack...!

It ate into the space Raijinki occupied as something began creeping out of it.

"What is that...?!" Blackas growled.

It was...a single arm. A human limb burst out of the emptiness and grabbed Raijinki by the neck.

"Lord Magnus...!"

"I know...!"

Sensing the encroaching danger, Leonis struck.

"Vira Zuo, Sharianos, Al Gu Belzelga!" He fired a series of eighth-order spells, each of them of a different elemental affinity.

Boooooom...!

The spells hit their target directly, yet...

"...It did nothing...?!" Leonis gritted his teeth.

The arm thrust out of the tear in space wasn't injured one bit.

Graaaaaaaaaaaaaah!

Raijinki let out a pained howl as the hand tightened around its neck...and then its massive, lightning-clad form was dragged into the tear.

"Lord Magnus... It approaches...!" Blackas warned.

The Sakura Orchid's god had vanished, and the crack where it once was grew larger. And then, something new appeared, emerging from the tear in space.

"...Ooh... Ohhhhhhhhh■■■■!"

It looked as if the lower portion of a gigantic animal had been stitched to the upper body of a human. The half-beast monster had eight arms and eight legs, golden shining hair, and pale, handsome, chiseled features.

"It can't be...!" Leonis breathed in disbelief, standing motionless.

He recognized the upper half of the creature.

"...So you, too... Even you have been reduced to a Void."

He should have considered that possibility. Both the Archsage Arakael Degradios and the Holy Woman Tearis Resurrectia had become Voids, so the fact this one was the same should not have been a surprise.

It was the strongest among the Six Heroes, the Swordmaster— Shardark Shin Ignis.

"...This will be the seventh time we've met in battle, master," Leonis whispered, his hand still tight on the Staff of Sealed Sins.

◆

"Hrahhhhhhhhhhhhh!" Riselia cried as she charged ahead.

She jumped, releasing the mana she'd gathered in her legs to go higher. The Bloody Sword glinted red as it plunged down on the Voids.

One of the giant's arms was sent flying.

"—■■■■■■■■!"

The Void let out a frenzied howl and thrashed about, easily crushing two shadow wolves biting into its leg underfoot. Its attack hurled a powerful surge of air at Riselia, and the young woman had to drop down to dodge it.

"Blood Chain!"

Infusing her own blood with mana, Riselia hurled it around another one of the Void's arms. After taking a breath, she struck with her Holy Sword, delivering a horizontal slash that flashed in the dark.

However, it still wasn't enough to kill the monstrous creature.

...It's tough. More so than an ogre class...

Typically, only an entire platoon working together could reliably defeat Voids of this level. Only Sakuya or the highest-ranking seniors at the academy could beat an opponent like this alone.

I have to at least make sure it doesn't hurt anyone.

Riselia was the only one around to defend the civilians in the shelter. This wasn't like six years ago. She had the power to do something now.

The Void swung its massive arm down with all the strength it could muster. It split the ground, sending blocks of construction material flying every which way.

"Pierce through all, dark lightning—Ivi Ire!"

Riselia jumped away and hurled a spell she'd only recently

learned. This was going to be a prolonged battle, so her best bet was to whittle away at her opponent with hit-and-away tactics.

...I have to protect the shelter on my own until the platoons from the academy get here.

The gigantic Void brought up an arm and howled.

"—Huh?!" Riselia's eyes widened in disbelief.

Particles of light gathered in the Void's hand, forming a massive battle-ax.

"The Void just created a weapon?!"

A Void capable of conjuring an armament. Excalibur Academy had no records of anything like it. And what's more, it almost looked like...

Like a Holy Sword...!

No, it couldn't have been. Holy Swords didn't give off that oily vapor. However, Riselia recalled encountering something similar recently.

Liat's Demon Sword...!

The Void with the ax rushed toward her.

It's quick!

It closed the distance in the blink of an eye and struck with its weapon. Riselia tried to deflect it with the Bloody Sword, but...

"...Kuh, aaah...!"

The sheer force of her opponent's blow sent her flying back. The Void gave chase, attacking with a horizontal sweep. The blade of the ax burned in red, firing a wave of flames that rushed over Riselia.

Riselia swiftly thrust the Bloody Sword into the ground, covering her entire body with blades of blood that glinted crimson.

When the young woman emerged, she was wearing the True Ancestor's Dress, a legend-class item given to her by Leonis. Riselia's silvery hair shone with mana as she thrust out her left hand. A magic circle formed at her palm.

"I'll blow you away—Di Farga!"

This was the most potent second-order spell Riselia could use at present. A scarlet flash erupted, canceling out the wave of flames. However, the Void didn't stop its advance.

"Ahhhhhhhhhhhhhhhhhh!" Riselia's entire body glowed brightly with mana.

Gripping the Bloody Sword with both hands, she blocked the incoming ax.

"...Back...off!"

Her arms went numb. The True Ancestor's Dress came with a price. Although it significantly bolstered the wearer's physical prowess, it consumed a great deal of mana in exchange. In other words, she had to defeat this Void quickly, or she would undoubtedly lose.

This is no normal Void...! Riselia bit her lip, just barely avoiding its flurry swings.

The giant Void moved like a masterful warrior.

"Hyahhhhhhhhh!" After evading the Void's many attacks, Riselia lunged at its flank.

"Bloom like a brilliant flower—Blood Vein!"

Mana filled the Bloody Sword, its edge emanating crimson light. Countless blades of blood manifested to shred the Void.

...I'll overwhelm it this way!

Her True Ancestor's Dress fluttering, Riselia drove another blow deep into the Void's core. However...

"—■■■■■■■■!"

The Void howled and brought its ax down again. Intense flames surged toward Riselia. As a member of the undead, Riselia was exceedingly weak to fire. Even her status as a Vampire Queen did not free her from that weakness.

"...!"

She forcibly avoided the attack by propelling herself away with mana. Scorching tongues licked at the air before her. If the blaze spread, she'd have nowhere to run.

No good!

Just as it seemed the flames were about to consume Riselia—

A streak cut across the battlefield.

Boooooooom!

An explosion blew sediment and rubble into the air, stopping the fire.

"...!"

Looking up, Riselia saw a brightly glowing Eye of the Witch orb floating overhead.

"Miss Finé!"

"I'll cover for you, Selia!"

The orb rotated and fired another flash of light at the Void. The searing beam struck the monster on the arm gripping the ax.

Now's my chance!

Riselia rushed through the rising smoke. She channeled her Vampire Queen mana into the Bloody Sword and—

"Blood Blade!"

All of her power released at once. A storm of red swords swirled around the giant Void's body. Its massive form finally toppled over with a loud thud.

"Haah, haah, haah... You saved me back there, Miss Finé," Riselia thanked her, catching her breath.

"I never thought I'd see Voids using Demon Swords..." Elfiné remarked.

Crack...!

The sound of shattering glass filled the area.

"...?!" Riselia looked up.

A massive fissure ran through the skies above the Seventh Assault Garden.

"Such an immense fracture in reality!"

Riselia had seen one that large only once before. It had been six years ago, right before the Stampede that destroyed the Third Assault Garden...

"—■■■■■■■■!"

And suddenly, the Void they'd just felled opened its eyes and screamed.

"...It's still alive?!"

Riselia immediately held up her Holy Sword, but the Void simply jumped away and landed atop a nearby building. It then began sprinting for the Central Garden.

"Selia, all the Voids in Old Town have started toward the same place," Elfiné said.

"What? Why?!"

"I don't know, either. But something's definitely happening in the Central Garden..."

Riselia suddenly felt her heart thumping ominously. She had a bad feeling about this.

"Miss Finé, I'm going to the Central Garden!"

"Huh? Selia, wait...!"

But Riselia had already left.

◆

Shardark Void Lord, the Swordmaster of the Six Heroes, had emerged from the tear in reality. He had devoured the Sakura Orchid's deity, Fuujinki, and merged with one of the Dark Lords, Dizolf Zoa, the Lord of Rage. After transforming so many times, he looked completely different than he had nine years ago. All that remained of his original body was his face, and even that was incomplete. One of his eyes had been crushed and was missing.

And now this monster had absorbed the other Sakura Orchid deity into himself. Standing atop a nearby laminated building was Setsura, patiently waiting for the Void Lord to completely emerge.

She took out a triangular black crystal from her white garb's sleeve. This was a Trapezohedron—a shard of the goddess had that perished one thousand years ago. On its own, it was nothing but a stone without any mana.

But should it be placed in a compatible vessel, it could become a receptacle for the goddess's soul.

Setsura's role was to beckon Shardark of the Six Heroes and turn him into a vessel for the goddess. The Kenki Gathering—or rather, their Demon Swords—were to be the sacrifice for her.

However, the plan had veered off course. Shardark was locked in combat with someone, that masked man she had fought earlier.

A wielder of sorcery, an ancient art said to have gone extinct centuries ago.

During their clash, he'd loosed one powerful spell after another. Nefakess had warned Setsura that someone capable of destroying the Archsage Arakael was hiding in the Seventh Assault Garden...

Either way, now that those two monsters were locked in battle, she couldn't so much as approach them. Thus, her only recourse was to wait with the shard of the goddess in hand.

However, she soon detected someone approaching from behind.

"Sister..."

Setsura turned around. A girl in priestess attire stood before her, Holy Sword at the ready. It was Sakuya Sieglinde, her younger sibling. Changed as they both were, each girl bore a striking resemblance to the other.

"—I was under the impression you were too injured to move," Setsura commented.

"I struck a deal," Sakuya replied.

"A deal?"

Whatever the answer, Sakuya was content not to give it. She only raised her Holy Sword.

Setsura decided to inquire about something else. "How did you know where I was?"

"I *saw* it," Sakuya replied.

"...?"

Sakuya lifted her bangs, revealing her left eye, which was now an amber shade.

"That eye—" Setsura said.

Before she could finish, however, Sakuya disappeared in a flash of lightning.

CHAPTER 10

HOLY SWORD AWAKENING

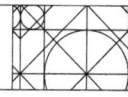

"—You've changed quite a bit since I last saw you, master."

A disfigured monster who had once been hailed as one of humanity's greatest champions had appeared from the tear in reality. His lower half was an amalgamation of gods, and all that remained of his original body was his handsome face.

"Looks like the eye I crushed is still missing."

Surely he could have regenerated it with ease. There must have been a reason he didn't. Leonis had no way of knowing what it was, though.

"Grohhhh... Grohhhhhhhhhhhh...!"

This ruler of the emptiness seemingly noticed Leonis, who was standing on a rooftop.

"Huh...? He recognizes me?"

The Archsage Arakael Degradios had identified Leonis, despite losing his mind to the nothingness. Perhaps Shardark still recalled his old nemesis, too.

—*No. That doesn't appear to be the case.*

The defunct hero's singular eyeball lacked awareness. It only acknowledged the massive presence of the Undead King as a threat and reacted instinctively.

A chance meeting between the Undead King and the Swordmaster of the Six Heroes. Had someone orchestrated this?

As far as Leonis could tell, no such person was around.

"Maybe it's fate that has led to our reunion, master." Leonis smirked under his mask as he aimed the Staff of Sealed Sins at the hulking Void Lord. "The time has come for me to take revenge. For the destruction of Necrozoa. For my many retainers, who died at your hand. For a thousand-year-old grudge!"

Leonis chanted his greatest destruction spell—the Dark Burst Flare, Arzam.

Booooooooooom!

The air trembled. An aura of darkness ruptured, consuming the surrounding buildings.

"Hmph. Perhaps it was too strong a wake-up call—what?!"

A flickering, radiant barrier surrounded Shardark, rendering even a destruction spell of the highest order completely useless. There wasn't so much as a speck of soot on him.

"...Holy element sorcery?!" Leonis gaped.

So that's how he stopped my earlier attacks...

"This is odd," Blackas growled. "I thought the Swordmaster never used any magic."

Leonis nodded. "You're right. He didn't. He always relied on his sword arm and nothing else."

"Has he consumed some sorcery powers...?"

The Six Heroes were ultimate life-forms, capable of eternal evolution and growth. Much like how the Archsage had merged with the immortal Holy Tree, Shardark must have claimed some servant of the gods capable of wielding powerful magic.

"Very well, then. I need only continue to hammer you with spells until your mana runs out!" Leonis declared with a sneer.

"Lord Magnus, I don't think that's a gamble you should take," Blackas warned him.

"How so?"

"Have you forgotten that your body is human now?"

"..."

His trusted companion's admonition made Leonis hesitate. Indeed, Leonis had failed his reincarnation and was now in the body he'd possessed as a young hero, meaning his mana capacity was far less than his reign as the Undead King.

Had Leonis been at his full strength, his spell would've pierced Shardark's barrier regardless of its resistance to dark sorcery.

"I can't believe that I, of all people, am falling short in magic...," Leonis lamented.

"—Look out!" Blackas cried.

Shardark's eight arms shone, each of them manifesting a weapon.

"Four swords, a spear, a bow, a scythe, and a shield—all of them legend-class armaments."

The spear crackled with lightning, and one of the swords was robed in wind. They had undoubtedly belonged to the Sakura Orchid deities Raijinki and Fuujinki.

"*Grohhhhhhhhhhhh!*" Shardark howled, and he threw the spear.

"Blackas!" Leonis grabbed on to the black wolf's mane.

Kzzzzzzzzzzzzzzzzzzzzzz!

The electrified polearm pierced the building Leonis and Blackas had been standing on, carving a giant hole through it. The structure began to fall apart like a landslide.

"He just threw a legend-class weapon like it was nothing...!" Leonis observed.

"Don't talk, Lord Magnus, lest you bite your tongue—" Blackas said, hopping between the falling bits of rubble like stepping-stones.

"Farga!" Leonis fired a fourth-order destruction spell above him, destroying nearby debris to form a smokescreen.

Whooosh!

A massive object sped right past him.

"What?!"

Boooooooooom...!

That heavy object struck the ground, producing a tremendous explosion.

...The reckless fool just threw the Aegis—a hero-class shield—at me!

The Six Heroes were a gathering of monsters, but he really stood head and shoulders above them.

Calling this monster the Swordmaster seems entirely inappropriate...!

Shardark had been known for his blade skills, but he was a master of all weapons.

Blackas landed on the ground and continued running, avoiding pieces of the collapsing building all the while. If they were to stop even once, one of the enemy's weapons would skewer them.

And no doubt those aren't the only armaments he's got...

"Lord Magnus, even I can't keep running forever...!" Blackas stated.

"—I know." Leonis scowled beneath his mask.

A siren blared through the urban area. All citizens had evacuated underground when Raijinki appeared in the sky, but the problem was Excalibur Academy. If they were to send out a force of Holy Swordsmen, they would take overwhelming losses.

Dáinsleif might be capable of slaying him in one blow, but...

It was Leonis's trump card, but it was not without flaw. Drawing the Demon Sword would drain Leonis's mana in seconds, so he had to make sure he used it only when he was confident it would end the fight.

The problem was that his opponent was Shardark.

...He's not like that potted plant, Arakael.

The Void Lord hurled another weapon at Leonis, this time an ax. Its spinning blade mowed down the buildings and then stuck into the ground.

Boooooooooom!

It must have connected with a mana supply line hidden below the ground because there was a blinding explosion.

...The way this is going, I have no other choice. I have to use it.

Leonis removed his Dark Lord's mask and overcoat, revealing his academy uniform. This wasn't an opponent he could beat while concealing his mana.

"Do you recognize my face, master?" he shouted toward the sky.

He'd hoped Shardark might react, but the monster's face didn't so much as flinch.

"...Tch, he's completely corrupted. At least Arakael recognized me..."

Leonis reached for the handle of the Staff of Sealed Sins. Wielding the Demon Sword would severely damage the Seventh Assault Garden, but there was no other option.

Letting go of Blackas's mane, Leonis landed on the ground.

Thou Art the Sword to Save the World, Gifted by the Heavens.

Thou Art the Sword to Ruin the World, Made to Rebel Against the Heavens.

Leonis slowly made to draw the Demon Sword—

"...What?!"

—but something kept him from doing so.

"What's wrong, Lord Magnus...?!" Blackas asked him, alarmed.

"Wh-why?! I can't...draw Dáinsleif!"

Leonis pulled as hard as he could, but the Demon Sword simply wouldn't come free of its scabbard.

"—It's attacking again, Lord Magnus!"

A flaming sword came cutting through the air, hurtling toward him!

◆

"Hahhhhhhhhhhhh!"

With a flash of lightning, Sakuya swung Raikirimaru.

Clangggggg!

Setsura blocked the blindingly swift diagonal slash with her own katana.

"Don't bother," she told Sakuya. "You cannot beat me."

"We'll see about that...!"

Sakuya took another step forward, attacking again. Sparks flew as their blades met.

"Impudent...!" Setsura snarled.

Her Holy Sword shone, and a demonic wind enveloped its blade.

...I see it. Over there!

Sakuya focused on the mystic eye of time. Amber light shone from it, and the world suddenly branched off. Her nerves' transmission speed accelerated rapidly, stretching a moment out into infinity. As everything moved in slow motion, a massive amount of information coursed into the young woman's mind—future possibilities unfurled before her.

Four led to certain death, but there was one outcome where

she survived. Within a world where one second became millions, Sakuya grasped that sole potentiality.

As the guards of their weapons rubbed against one another, Sakuya lowered herself and *released her katana.*

"What?!" Setsura exclaimed in clear disbelief.

An outburst of demonic wind cut through the air, but Sakuya had evaded it entirely. She dove to Setsura's flank and extended a hand—

"Come, Raikirimaru!" she called to her Holy Sword, which was still in mid-fall.

A magnetic charge ran through her fingers, drawing the weapon back into her grip. Sakuya took a step forward and struck.

"...!"

The tip of her blade caught Setsura's cheek. Sakuya took another step and cut diagonally.

...!

Again, Sakuya *saw* it. Two possible deaths this time. Setsura vanished, leaving an afterimage. With a sound like a hurricane, she appeared at Sakuya's back. Had the younger sister not moved her body slightly aside, her throat would have been pierced through. Sakuya kicked off the ground to jump back as Setsura swung her Holy Sword down, firing a sharp blast of air.

Kuh...!

Ignoring the searing pangs in her left eye, Sakuya called upon its power again. By slightly twisting her body, she evaded seven potential demises.

...I can't control this eye properly.

Using it frequently was almost too much for her mind to bear. Sakuya decided she had to limit the use of the mystic eye to critical moments.

Unfortunately, every arc of Setsura's katana was certain death.

"—How are you still alive?" the older sister demanded.

"...I should be the one asking that question," replied the younger.

"With your sword skills, I should have landed a fatal blow on you three times already, yet you keep finding ways to cling to life," Setsura declared, evidently perplexed. "Aren't you going to use your Demon Sword?"

"I'm saving it for when I need it," Sakuya lied.

Yamichidori's power was no good here. She needed Raikirimaru, with its power of acceleration, to use this mystic eye to its fullest extent. Even if she could predict the future, it wouldn't be of any help if she didn't have the speed to react. She covered her throbbing left eye with a hand. She could use it only one more time before reaching her limit.

"You underestimate me," Setsura stated coldly, raising her katana overhead.

Its blade shone bright, calling a howling storm around it.

"Mikagami-style swordsmanship—Demonic Gale Slash!"

Setsura vanished—and the next moment, the blade was right before Sakuya's eyes.

◆

Booooooooom!

The flaming sword tore into the ground, producing a powerful explosion. Leonis immediately called up a barrier spell, defending himself from the raging flames.

"...This is bad," he hissed, the Staff of Sealed Sins tight in his hand.

Why couldn't he draw out Dáinsleif?

His gaze then fell to the countless weapons thrust into the ground. An alarming possibility occurred to him.

...It can't be!

If Shardark devoured gods and took their weapons...

"...You! Don't tell me you devoured a Dark Lord?!" Leonis exclaimed at the enemy above.

If Shardark had, it only made sense that Leonis couldn't wield Dáinsleif against him. Same as how he couldn't use its power against Veira, the Dragon Lord...

The goddess had placed a restriction on Dáinsleif, forbidding its power from being used against other Dark Lords.

Damn it... Which of you fools got consumed?!

Leonis was furious—not at Shardark, but at the Dark Lord who had been absorbed. Was it Gazoth, the Lord of Beasts, or perhaps Dizolf, the Lord of Rage? Surely it couldn't have been the Lord of the Seas.

...No, that doesn't matter right now!

If Leonis couldn't rely on Dáinsleif, he would need to use one of the Arc Seven, but Zolgstar Mezekis had been damaged in the battle with Veira. There was always the option of awakening his third minion, but that was liable to make things worse. There wasn't enough time to undo the seal anyway.

Shardark landed on the ground.

"...?!"

The Void Lord's eight horse-like legs collided hard with the shattered street. The pressure he exuded was intense enough that Leonis felt it from a fair distance. The boy felt beads of cold sweat run down his chin.

This can't be... I, the mighty Undead King, greatest of Dark Lords, am feeling fear...

Leonis felt a sardonic grin spread across his face.

...Do I stand a chance? Can I defeat this monster?

Leonis Death Magnus was by no means undefeated. In his

earliest days as the Undead King, he was the weakest of the Dark Lords. His mana capacity far eclipsed the others, but he'd lost his power as a hero, and he'd had to create his underlings using necromancy.

He'd lacked the natural power the Dragon Lord and the Lord of Beasts possessed and the vast forces that the Lord of Rage commanded. At the time, Rivaiz Deep Sea had unquestionably been the best Dark Lord.

However, with each defeat, Leonis rose from the grave mightier than he had been. He would learn more sorcery, greedily hoarding wisdom and strengthening his minions. Nothing was more fearsome than a fully matured undead.

Those many years of experience informed Leonis that this was a fight he could not win.

"Lord Magnus, we must retreat for now," Blackas advised.

"..."

Leonis remained where he was, however, still holding on to his staff. Retreating now would mean abandoning the Seventh Assault Garden to its fate. To discard the land he'd designated as his kingdom would be to discard Dáinsleif—and the last wish Roselia Ishtaris had left in the Demon Sword.

The scene of Necrozoa's defeat to the human armies surfaced in Leonis's mind. And then he saw the eighteenth platoon, the orphanage's children, the Demon Wolf Pack...and finally, Riselia, his minion.

"Grohhhhhhhhhhhhhhhhhhhhhhhhhh!"

Shardark howled. Voids climbed endlessly through the tear in the sky. It was just like the Stampede from a few months ago and the catastrophe that had destroyed the Sakura Orchid...

Leonis took a sharp breath.

"I will not retreat, Blackas."

"…"

"I am the Dark Lord that reigns over this kingdom."

"…I see," Blackas replied, raising his head and fixing his golden eyes on Leonis. "Then I shall accompany you, too."

"Thank you, old friend…"

Blackas became a mass of dark flames that enveloped Leonis. This was a unique spell called Black Tyrant. It was magic that allowed Leonis to significantly increase his own physical attributes by taking in Blackas's power.

Holding up his staff, Leonis spoke to Shardark. "—Come, greatest hero of humanity. The Undead King will be your opponent."

◆

The moment the blade of demonic wind was about to tear into Sakuya's heart—

"Mikagami-style swordsmanship—Lightning Flash!"

Sakuya slashed at the future her mystic eye indicated. At the point where countless future possibilities converged—

"Kuh, aaah…!"

She managed to evade the katana trained on her heart by rotating so that it tore into her shoulder instead. And Setsura was…

"…So we ended up…cutting one another…," Sakuya whispered into her sister's ear, making the older girl's crimson eyes go wide with fear.

Raikirimaru's blade had stabbed Setsura's chest. Or rather, *into the black crystal hidden beneath her white Sakura Orchid clothes.*

"…This whole time…that's what you were aiming for?" Setsura asked.

Sakuya nodded. Her mystic eye gave her a glimpse of a future where her sister offered up that black crystal to the Void Lord, only for her to be swallowed by him. She knew she couldn't let that happen.

Sakuya hadn't come to kill her sibling, but to save her.

"Kuh... Aah...!"

Grasping onto her wounded shoulder, Sakuya faltered and fell. Raikirimaru slipped from her hand and dissolved into motes of light.

"—Fool," Setsura spat. Her previously expressionless face was twisted with vexation. "You clung to life by way of a miracle, and yet you chose to cast it away like this..."

She reached out, grabbing Sakuya by the throat.

"Kuh... Ahhhhhhhhhhhhhhhhhh!"

A red glint shone in Setsura's eyes. Her fingers dug into Sakuya's neck.

"I won't grant you an easy death. Become an undead minion instead—"

"Se...tsura..."

But just then, the air screeched with a whipping sound, and Setsura's arm went flying through the air.

...Huh?

With nothing to support her weight, Sakuya collapsed to the ground.

"This swordswoman already belongs to my master. You will not lay another hand on her," a lovely voice, as clear as glass, declared. The petite figure stood up atop the building's water tower, looking down at the scene. "I could face you in her stead, if you'd like. Though I'm probably stronger than you are."

It was hard to make out this new combatant's face in the dark. But judging by the way she was dressed...

...A maid?

What was someone like that doing here?

"..."

Setsura gazed fixedly at the intruder...and then turned on her heel, stepping away from Sakuya.

"Sister!" Sakuya called out, grasping helplessly after.

But Setsura did not stop. She faded into the darkness without so much as a parting glance.

◆

Shardark hurled himself at Leonis, the steel floor of the building they were in rumbling with each step of his eight massive legs. His body was coated in sizzling lightning, likely the product of Raijinki's divine power.

"Eighth-order, tactical-level spell—Graz Garud!" Leonis struck the ground with the bottom of his staff.

Circular pillars of rock appeared in thin air, crushing Shardark from every direction.

His light barrier shouldn't be able to block a purely physical attack spell. However...

"Grohhhhhhhhhhhhhhhhhhhhhhhhhhhhh!"

Shardark shattered the stone prison with a howl and continued his charge as if nothing had been in his way.

...Such brute strength!

Leonis clicked his tongue and quickly cast more magic.

"Sixth-order spell—Belze Farga!"

This magic fired bursts of the fourth-order spell, Farga, in quick succession. Countless white-hot balls of fire buffeted Shardark in a sequence of explosions. Unsurprisingly, sorcery of that caliber wasn't enough to harm the Void Lord. However, Leonis's true intention was to use the blast to cause the structure around them to fall. As Shardark froze up from the attack, the building's gigantic mass came crashing down.

Crrrrrrrrrrsssshhhhhhhhhh!

"Though I brought it to bear on you, humans built this edifice. Surely even a hero won't walk away from that unscathed."

The rumbling collapse kicked up a great cloud of dust, but Leonis wasted no time.

"Tenth-order destruction spell—Zemexis Jyura!"

Small asteroids appeared from nowhere, pummeling Shardark as he remained buried under the rubble.

Boom, boom, boom, boooooooom!

"...Haah, haah, haah... What?!" There wasn't even enough time for Leonis to catch his breath.

Shardark was already rising from the smoke and dust. He was visibly injured, but none of it was substantial enough to be a hindrance.

"You monster...!"

Before Leonis had time for another spell, Shardark effortlessly threw a sword of wind at him. The godly weapon came flying, forming a whirlwind that kicked up debris.

...A sword endowed with the power of demonic wind. I can't avoid it.

Leonis immediately thrust the Staff of Sealed Sins ahead and met the spinning blade with the staff's handle.

Screeeeeeeeeeeeeeeeeeech!

The dark flames around his body—Black Tyrant—surged violently.

"...Nng... Kuh, aaaaaaah!"

Ultimately, he failed to deflect the attack.

The air burst, and Leonis was blown away and landed hard against the ground.

"Khhk... Hah..."

His fragile body would have died from the impact had it not been for Black Tyrant's power.

This is...pathetic...

Shardark drew more legend-class weapons from the emptiness and prepared to hurl one, a gigantic lance, at the boy struggling to get to his feet.

"Hyahhhhhhhhhhhhhhhhhhhh!"

Suddenly, a red shadow descended from above and stabbed Shardark's arm with a sword.

"...Miss Selia?!" Leonis cried, astonished.

The young woman's argent hair shone brilliantly, and she was wearing a crimson dress.

"Leo, run...!" Riselia called out desperately.

The Bloody Sword's blade gave off scarlet light as it sank into the Void Lord's arm, and razors made of blood stabbed the monster. Unfortunately, an attack of that magnitude wasn't effective against Shardark. Riselia should have been no more than a fly to him, and yet—

"*Grohhhhhh... Grohhh... Grohhhhhhhhhhhhhhhhhhhhhh!*"

—the Swordmaster of the Six Heroes reacted to a startling degree.

"...G...oddess...Sel...ia...Ahhhhhhhhhhhhhhhhhhhhhhhhhh!"

...*What?*

Leonis frowned at Shardark's broken cry.

The Swordmaster had lost his mind to the emptiness, yet now he spoke.

And did he just say...goddess?

Shardark grabbed Riselia and then attempted to bury her within his own body.

"—Miss Selia!" Leonis shouted as he ran over.

Blast it all... He's trying to consume her, too?!

Leonis sprinted across the ruined street and through the clouds of dust. He had no plan. He was just running as the gears in his mind turned frantically. Magic didn't affect Shardark, and

Dáinsleif couldn't be drawn against a Dark Lord. Substantial physical attacks appeared effective to some degree, but what about large-scale destruction magic from close range? Or maybe curses?

There were hundreds of methods to kill a champion...but none of them would work against the mightiest of the Six Heroes!

"Le...o... Don't... R-run...!"

Half of Riselia's body had already sunken into Shardark's body.

—I won't make it in time...!

"Look at me, Swordmaster—Shardark Shin Ignis!" Leonis shouted.

As if from nowhere, a bright burst of light erupted from Leonis's hand, and he stopped in his tracks.

What...?

The luminous motes converged, manifesting as an object in his hand—one that greatly reminded him of something.

It resembled the weapon Riselia had used to battle the Voids in Necrozoa's underground mausoleum. This kind of tool hadn't existed during Leonis's era, and yet he now held what was unquestionably a pistol.

...This... It can't be. A Holy Sword?!

Holy Swords were a power that the planet granted humanity, allowing them to fight back against the Voids. And now one was sitting in his grip as comfortably as a sword he'd wielded for years. Its name was etched into the barrel in glowing letters—EXCALIBUR XX.

...A Dark Lord like me has awakened to the power of a Holy Sword?

Why now, at a time like this...? And why a pistol, a weapon Leonis had never so much as held?! There were many questions, but they would have to wait.

Mana began gathering at the top of the Holy Sword's muzzle, letting off a brilliant radiance.

Wait, this is... My mana, it's...dropping rapidly...

Leonis's vast reserves were being focused to that single point. Even if his magical power was only a third of what it had once been, he still possessed enough to cast high-level spells in quick succession.

If all that energy were condensed into one shot, just how much force would it have...?

Leonis could tell, instinctively, that this was a weapon to kill heroes.

He held the Holy Sword with both hands, fixing its sights between Shardark's eyes. All of his mana gathered at the muzzle, glowing bright enough to blot out all else.

This is all the strength I have. I can fire only one shot.

If this failed, he wouldn't get another chance.

Leonis steadied his breath and brought his finger to the trigger. Shardark turned to face him.

...He noticed me!

"*Grohhhhhhhhhhhhhhhhhhhhhhhhhhhhhhhhhhhh!*"

With Riselia's body still in his grip, the Void Lord ran toward Leonis. The boy gritted his teeth. Did he shoot? No, there was a chance he might hit Riselia. If he were as skilled as Regina, he might have been able to strike a moving target in the head, but...

But suddenly.

Multiple gigantic shadows burst into their battle and grappled the advancing Swordmaster.

"...What?!"

They were the gigantic Voids from Old Town. They swarmed Shardark and, with obvious intent, began to attack him.

"Grohhhhhhhhh...!"

The hero of the emptiness used his eight arms to swing his weapons about, slaughtering the Voids. However, the disruption did manage to keep him held in place.

Such was the tenacity of those seeking revenge for their ruined homeland. Now Leonis had a chance.

He pulled his Holy Sword's trigger, and the streak of light hit Shardark squarely between the eyes—

Crack...

—causing a small fracture to form in Shardark's forehead.

Crack... Crack... Crack...!

It expanded rapidly to cover the Void Lord's entire body. Shardark's arm was completely overtaken by the fissures, and Riselia fell to the ground.

"...Miss Selia!" Leonis called out as he collapsed.

With all of his mana exhausted, he couldn't manage to stay on his feet.

"...How...regrettable... The goddess's...vessel...within my...grasp..."

Shardark reached toward Riselia, but the hand crumbled away.

The vessel...? What is he saying?!

"Grohhhhhh... Grohhhhhh... Grohhhhhhhhhh...!"

The hero who had been consumed by nothingness howled loudly enough to shake the collapsed buildings. Fractures overtook his body, distorting the space around him.

The Swordmaster of the Six Heroes, still fighting against the Voids holding him back, disappeared into the tear in space.

EPILOGUE

"Miss Selia...Miss Selia, are you all right?!"

"Mm...Leo...?"

Leonis knelt beside her and gently shook her shoulders. Riselia's eyes opened but only barely.

"Hm... Where's the Void...?" she asked feebly.

"It disappeared into a crack," Leonis explained bitterly.

The tear in the skies above the Seventh Assault Garden was gradually closing, and the Voids that had appeared would be dispatched by Excalibur Academy's military units.

...So my seventh match with Shardark ended in a draw.

And yet Leonis's mana was nearly entirely depleted. If that battle had continued, he would have undoubtedly lost.

"...I see. Leo, I'm...I'm glad you're safe."

"Miss Selia, please don't do anything that reckless again... Still, thank you for rescuing me."

This was the second time she'd saved his life. Riselia smiled softly and took his hands in hers.

Leonis's Holy Sword had already disappeared. He didn't know how to summon it at will, so he'd have to ask Riselia about that later.

Still, to think that a Dark Lord like me would awaken to the power of a Holy Sword...

It wasn't that he hadn't considered the possibility, but it still came as a surprise. And why had it taken the form of a pistol? A Holy Sword was said to be a materialization of one's soul, so it should have been a staff, or perhaps a sword, owing to his time as a hero.

The Holy Swords were supposedly a power granted to humankind by the planet to oppose the Voids. Was that the truth, though? Why did Holy Swords and Voids suddenly appear sixty-four years ago? The fact Leonis now possessed a Holy Sword could've been a clue to solving the mystery.

The tear in the sky was gradually shrinking. Leonis felt confident that he would encounter Shardark Shin Ignis, the hero who had succumbed to the power of nothingness, again. As Leonis was now, however, he wouldn't be able to stop the man who had consumed gods and Dark Lords.

...I must hasten the reformation of the Dark Lords' Armies. And I think I've had quite enough of those fools who are skulking about and plotting behind the scenes.

Leonis turned his gaze to the sky and gave an indomitable smile.

—It's about time I move in to crush *them.*

◆

At the Former Veriad Continent, some 2,700 kilometers to the southwest, located 9,044 meters below sea level, was a point called the Oceanic Gulf. Within the inky dark of the water, a large crimson flame burned.

"...Honestly, did it have to sink so deep...?"

A stunningly beautiful girl with dazzling crimson hair sighed as she stood before a wrecked structure. It was the remains of the Azure Hold, which had fallen to an offensive led by Gisark, the Divine Dragon of the Six Heroes.

Veira hoped to use the astronomical observation device at the fort's core, the Almagest, to confirm changes in the position of the heavenly bodies during the last one thousand years, and possibly solve the mystery of the Star of Calamity.

Looking around the ruins, she spotted many gigantic dragon bones sunken in the structure. Veira closed her eyes, silently mourning the loss of brave dragons. And then...

"—Your queen returns!"

Thuuuuuuuuud!

She slammed her fist against the gate, blowing it off its frame. Then the Dark Lord ventured deeper into the wreckage, walking barefoot. The deepest parts of the ruins were protected by an ancient barrier that kept the seawater out.

"The Almagest should be just past here..."

Yet no sooner had Veira entered the throne room than she came to a stop.

"...Who's there?"

Someone was occupying the Dragon Lord's throne, as though they owned the place.

"Oh, I spy me a reckless fool. To take advantage of my absence and sit upon my chair—" Veira produced a red fireball in her hand. "I'm a forgiving Dark Lord, so I will burn you to nothing quickly."

The burning sphere streaked forward, melting the surrounding stone pillars.

Tiiiiiink!

However, they were easily extinguished before reaching the figure on the throne.

"...What?!" Veira's ruby eyes betrayed her disbelief.

In the dying light of the flames, she spied a girl with a cold beauty and hair the color of amethysts.

"...It can't be. Rivaiz Deep Sea, the Lord of the Seas?!"

AFTERWORD

Happy New Year, everyone. This is Yu Shimizu, happily delivering *The Demon Sword Master of Excalibur Academy*, Volume 6, to you. Thank you for your patience!

As the cover illustration implies, our tough-but-cute samurai girl, Sakuya, takes center stage this time around. The Void Lord who destroyed her homeland; her sister, who has been resurrected as an undead; the enigmatic being who granted her a Demon Sword—and of course, her encounters with the Dark Lord (who actually sleeps in the same dorm as her). Whatever will happen to her next...?!

I hope you're looking forward to how she uses her new power later in the story.

Now then, it's time for a bit of gratitude. A huge thank-you to Asagi Tosaka for drawing more wonderful illustrations! Both the color inserts and the black-and-white pictures are all of fantastic quality. I can only fall to my hands and knees in your presence!

To Asuka Keigen, who's in charge of the manga adaptation, I look forward to every issue you release. Thank you so much!

AFTERWORD

And of course, the biggest thanks go to all you readers for your support of the series! Our next volume will bring a new development in the story of the Dark Lord and the Holy Swords. Please look forward to it!

—*Yu Shimizu, January 2021*

HAVE YOU BEEN TURNED ON TO LIGHT NOVELS YET?

IN STORES NOW!

SWORD ART ONLINE, VOL. 1-24
SWORD ART ONLINE PROGRESSIVE 1-8

The chart-topping light novel series that spawned the explosively popular anime and manga adaptations!

MANGA ADAPTATION AVAILABLE NOW!

SWORD ART ONLINE © Reki Kawahara ILLUSTRATION: abec
KADOKAWA CORPORATION ASCII MEDIA WORKS

ACCEL WORLD, VOL. 1-25

Prepare to accelerate with an action-packed cyber-thriller from the bestselling author of *Sword Art Online*.

MANGA ADAPTATION AVAILABLE NOW!

ACCEL WORLD © Reki Kawahara ILLUSTRATION: HIMA
KADOKAWA CORPORATION ASCII MEDIA WORKS

SPICE AND WOLF, VOL. 1-22

A disgruntled goddess joins a traveling merchant in this light novel series that inspired the *New York Times* bestselling manga.

MANGA ADAPTATION AVAILABLE NOW!

SPICE AND WOLF © Isuna Hasekura ILLUSTRATION: Jyuu Ayakura
KADOKAWA CORPORATION ASCII MEDIA WORKS

IS IT WRONG TO TRY TO PICK UP GIRLS IN A DUNGEON?, VOL. 1–16

A would-be hero turns damsel in distress in this hilarious send-up of sword-and-sorcery tropes.

MANGA ADAPTATION AVAILABLE NOW!

Is It Wrong to Try to Pick Up Girls in a Dungeon? © Fujino Omori / SB Creative Corp.

ANOTHER

The spine-chilling horror novel that took Japan by storm is now available in print for the first time in English—in a gorgeous hardcover edition.

MANGA ADAPTATION AVAILABLE NOW!

Another © Yukito Ayatsuji 2009 / KADOKAWA CORPORATION, Tokyo

A CERTAIN MAGICAL INDEX, VOL. 1–22

Science and magic collide as Japan's most popular light novel franchise makes its English-language debut.

MANGA ADAPTATION AVAILABLE NOW!

A CERTAIN MAGICAL INDEX © Kazuma Kamachi
ILLUSTRATION: Kiyotaka Haimura
KADOKAWA CORPORATION ASCII MEDIA WORKS

VISIT YENPRESS.COM TO CHECK OUT ALL THE TITLES IN OUR NEW LIGHT NOVEL INITIATIVE AND...

GET YOUR YEN ON!

www.YenPress.com